FIND ME IN PASSION

A DARK PES NOVELLA

MAL & CA (PART 3)

BY JENNER

CHAPTER 1

*P*AIN.

 It is like a living thing, moving around me.
Through me.

 Hot wires that slice flesh, that pulverize bone.

 Torment rising, torture pushing.

 Filling me. Hurting me.

 And though I try to turn it off—to hide inside myself
someplace deep where the pain cannot get to me—it is
futile.

 Another wave of agony tears through me, and I try to
fight. I try to run.

 But I am bound here, lashed to a wooden post.
Forced to do nothing but stand and endure.

 Stand, and fight the weapon inside me.

 But I won't be able to fight much longer.

I can feel it—a wild power rising. A violent explosion.

A weapon, hidden inside me against my will.

A weapon that I have tried to learn to control. But I know now that I have failed, because no matter how much I fight, the power just builds and builds and builds, and I can feel my body heating. My skin tingling with the force that is going to burst out of me.

I cannot do this alone.

I cannot do this at all.

I cry out for Malcolm—I need his help. I need his strength.

But he is not here. They've taken me.

This is it. This is the end.

And as that horrible truth tears through me—as the fire starts to burst out of me—I scream and I scream and I scream.

CHAPTER 2

"CHRISTINA! *CHRISTINA!*"

I open my eyes, my body tense, my heart pounding so hard in my chest that I fear I will crack a rib.

At first, I can see nothing. Just a blood red haze of fear. Then my vision clears, and there he is.

Mal.

The relief that sweeps over me is palpable. Mal is here, and that means that I am safe.

I look at him, cherishing the sight of him. His face is chiseled perfection softened only by the shadow of beard stubble on his jaw and chin. His dark hair gleams in the pale glow of street lamps filtering in through the window. Even here in bed he appears calm. In control. A man certain of himself and his surroundings.

Only his stormy gray eyes reveal his worry.

I wrap my arms around him and hold him tight. My love. My mate. The man I have known for thousands of years.

The lover I am only beginning to know again.

My face is buried against his shoulder, and I breathe deep as the remnants of the nightmare fall away. He is shirtless, and his skin is warm against my cheek. The lingering scent of soap from our shower before bed soothes me, and I keep my eyes closed, hoping that the longer he holds me, the more distant the dream will become.

Tenderly, he tips my head back, then looks into my eyes. As always, I am awed and humbled by the depth of emotion I see on his face. By the intense passion that is directed solely at me. "You're fine," he says. "You're safe."

"I know." My words are thin. "I do."

He strokes my cheek, then kisses me softly. "You've had nightmares for two nights now. What can I do?"

"Right now, just hold me."

"I'm already doing that."

I nod, because he is. And in his arms, I do feel safe. But even Mal cannot soothe my deepest fears. Because I know too well what is inside of me.

More, I know that it cannot be controlled, no matter how badly both of us might wish otherwise.

There is only one way to make sure that the weapon inside me causes no harm, and that is to kill me.

At the thought, I tremble in his arms.

"Tell me," he whispers. "Tell me the dream so that I can help."

When I don't answer, he strokes my hair. "Was it me? Did I come to you? Did I kill you?"

The pain in his voice rips me up inside. "Don't," I say. "Don't ever feel guilty for doing what you had to do."

I mean the words, and I know he understands, but that doesn't erase the torment or the sadness I see in his eyes. And for that, I can hardly blame him. Had our positions been reversed, I don't know how I could have survived the long years of torture. The horror that started over three thousand years ago.

We'd come to this world accidentally. Mal and I and all the other members of the Phoenix Brotherhood. We'd left our own world to chase a vile enemy who had stolen a horrific weapon with the power to destroy the very fabric of the universe. But an accident had steered us off course, the brotherhood and our prey. We'd been thrust into this dimension, this world.

And though we had left our home as creatures of pure, sentient energy, this dimension cannot support such life, and we found new form in willing humans, merging with them and becoming immortal in the process.

But while the brotherhood's new form was acquired peaceably, our prey's form was not. The fuerie did not merge, but took. Possessing humans, burning out their souls, and using the bodies for their own dark purposes.

And one such purpose was to hide the weapon. Like us, it had to be bound in this world. So the fuerie assaulted and took me, and then made me their vessel for the weapon.

Mal and the rest of our team fought to rescue me, but it was too late. The damage was done. And when Mal realized the nature of what had been done to me—when it became clear that I couldn't control the weapon inside me—he did the only thing that he could do.

He killed me.

He killed me to save me. To save the world.

At the time that he did it, he believed that I would come back to him. We were immortal creatures, after all, and I should have been born again in the phoenix fire.

But the weapon had changed me, and I did not come back. Not for many hundreds of years, until I was reincarnated into the body of an Egyptian girl.

And, once again, I carried the burden of the destructive power that hid deep inside me, though I did not know it. And I didn't remember Mal, either.

Once again Mal did his duty. And again after that and again and again and again.

He killed me so many times throughout the

ages that it is a miracle he was not driven mad.

But in the end, he could do it no more.

This time, when I came back, I remembered him. Not all of it—hardly anything, really. But enough that I knew him. That I could say his name.

And that was all it took.

He defied his duty.

He risked the world.

He brought me home.

And though I am horrified by and terrified of this weapon inside me, I know that Mal has had the harder time of it.

"It wasn't you in the dream," I say, finally answering his question. "It was just me. Me and the weapon and the pain."

"Tell me."

I look at him. "It was like the last time. I was tied to a pole. And they were hurting me." My voice starts to rise and crack with the memory. "And the pain made the weapon bubble up in me. And I couldn't stop it—I couldn't—"

"Shhh." He presses a finger to my lips, and just that simple touch calms my panic. "You're safe. It was just a dream."

"This time."

I see the shadow on his face, and regret my words.

"Christina..."

"No. Mal, I—" But I can't find the right words to soothe him, and so I just kiss him. Soft at first, and then hard and desperate as the need rises in both of us.

There has always been passion between us, but it is different now—a combination of familiar comfort and new discovery. Because though we both wish it were not true, my memories have not fully returned. And even if they had, I cannot deny that I am different than I was.

I have lived hundreds of lives, and the imprint of all the women I have been is now part of me. Over the last few days, I've been remembering bits and pieces of them. Slave girls and noblewomen, mothers and sisters, criminals and even a saint. Now, I am Jaynie. Jaynie Hart, who grew up with a crazy mother who told her the devil lived inside her.

Jaynie Hart, who was always more comfortable playing a role.

Jaynie Hart, who still isn't sure if she is Jaynie or Christina or someone else entirely. The one thing I am sure of is that the only place I feel truly safe—truly *me*—is in Mal's arms.

I pull back, breaking our kiss, my lips tingling. I meet his eyes and see the heat there along with the question. I want to tell him that I am fine. I'm good. At least for right now, with him, there is nothing else that I need.

The words don't come. Instead, all I can manage is his name, low and rough with passion. "*Mal.*" It is a plea. A prayer. And he does not disappoint.

In one wild, violent move, he covers me, laying me out flat on the huge bed that dominates the master bedroom in his six-story brownstone. I gasp, surprised by the unexpected motion, but also overwhelmed by the feel of him, naked and hard and heavy on top of me.

Like him, I am wearing nothing, and now I close my eyes and succumb to the glorious sensation of skin against skin. His entire body is warm, as if he generates heat like a furnace, and I writhe with pleasure as his hands stroke me, sliding over my skin and easing up my rib cage.

He cups my breasts, then teases my nipples with his thumbs, pinching lightly and sending hot coils of desire looping through me, firing my senses and pooling between my thighs.

I arch up, relishing the pressure of his erection against my lower abdomen, but wanting so much more than that. I shift my hips so that the hard length of his cock rubs against me, and I smile with satisfaction at his low moan of pleasure.

With my arms around his neck, I tilt my head up, only to be humbled by the look of adoration I see reflected on his face.

"Close your eyes," he whispers, "and tell me what you need."

His fingers still stroke me, and he trails kisses down my body.

I tremble under his touch, craving so much more than he can give me. I want him to take me all the way to the edge, yes. But I also want to go over—and that, we cannot do. Even now I can feel passion curling through me. Heating me. Boiling within me.

And soon, I know, we run the risk of boiling over.

"Mal. We can't. We—"

"Shhhh." He bends to brush a kiss over my lips. "Trust me," he says. "Trust me to take you as far as we can go, but no farther. Trust me to take you right to the edge and then hold on tight. Can you do that?" he asks as he slips his hand between my legs and strokes me.

I'm wet and open to him, and I gasp as his fingers enter me. "Can you?" he asks, his voice rough against my ear.

"Yes." My back arches up. Damn the risk; I want more. So much more. "Please."

"Please, what?"

"Don't stop. I want more."

Slowly he kisses his way down my body, leaving a tingling trail of desire his wake. "How much more?"

"Everything." My voice breaks as pleasure wars with need. And then, as he spreads my legs—as his fingers open me and the tip of his cock presses inside me—the churning sensations rise up again and need gives way to fear.

"No," I say as I press my thighs together then pull my knees up as I try to roll to my side. "Mal, please, no."

He is off me in a heartbeat, then at my side, his face so close to mine that I would have to be blind not to see his concern.

"What happened?" he asks. "You weren't there yet. Not even close." He strokes my cheek gently. "If we're going to practice control, we have to push the envelope, and you have trust that I won't let it go too far."

I shake my head. "I told you I needed everything. That I want everything. And I do, Mal, I really do. But don't you see? What I want, I can't have. And what I don't want is to be the Exploding Woman."

"Oh, lover." His voice is full of pain, and I know that it is all the worse for him because this is something he can't give me. That he can't fix. "That's why we're working on control, remember?"

I close my eyes as he pulls me tight against

him. "I don't want to have to work on it," I admit. I just want the pleasure of his touch. And I don't want to play games. Not unless those games are just for us.

Bottom line, I don't want the fate of the world tied to my romance with Mal.

And the truth is, I know that it isn't. Not really. Because while the weapon might trigger if I get too excited, teaching me control can only go so far toward saving us.

I open my eyes to find him focused on me, his brow furrowed with worry. "You're thinking very loud."

I smirk. "Sorry about that."

"Tell me what's on your mind."

I hesitate, then say boldly, "It won't work." He says nothing, so I continue on gamely. "I love the way you touch me. The way you make me feel. Controlling myself, holding back, submitting to your demands and instructions—it's exciting."

"But?"

"But that's all it is. Just lovers' games. It's not the way to win the battle, Mal. And it won't save the world."

"It will."

I shake my head. "They drugged me. I have no defense against that. All the control in the world won't help me battle back narcotics."

"But you have to be awake to trigger the weapon, and when they wake you, you can control it."

I smile sadly, then curl my fingers with his. "We both know I didn't control it—I *couldn't* control it. You took the brunt of it. You saved us, Mal. Me, you, the entire world. And if you hadn't been there..." I trail off, letting the words hang.

"It was too soon. But with more practice, more skill..."

I shift on the bed so that I am straddling him. I want to see his face. I want to touch him. I want him to understand what I'm saying. "I have no defense against that level of pain. It was brutal, Mal. Horrible."

I see him flinch, and I know that my words hurt him, too, but I press on, because it's important he understands. "What you've done— what we do—it makes sense, but it's not enough.

And you could up the ante, I know that. You could spank me, flog me. And I wouldn't object. Hell, even without the weapon and our training games, I wouldn't object," I finally say, admitting the secret desire I'd kept hidden. "But it wouldn't be enough. It wouldn't be nearly enough."

I see understanding in his eyes and continue. "Don't you see? What I'd want you to do doesn't go far enough. And what might be enough isn't something I'd be willing to do."

"It's okay," he says. "And it's not about the level of pain, but about control."

I make a face. "How much I hurt ties directly to how much control I have. And how long I can maintain it."

He slides out from under me so that he is sitting up in bed, leaving me beside his legs and facing him. I grab a pillow and hug it to me, both for warmth and because this conversation has left me feeling exposed, even to Mal.

"The truth is," he continues, "it's not really pain or control or even the weapon that are the issue."

"No?"

"Do you trust me?" he asks.

"Yes. Of course."

"Wholly and completely?"

"Yes." I frown, because I have told him this before.

"No, you don't."

"Dammit, Mal, you know that I—"

"Do you think I didn't see your face?"

I close my mouth, confused by his words. "My face? What, now?"

"Tonight, yes. And after the battle. After Asher agreed with me that it makes no sense to kill you. Even with the weapon, you're more use alive."

I hug the pillow tighter. A recent side effect of the weapon inside me is the unexpected but undeniably handy skill of seeing our enemy. And I mean literally seeing them spread out on a map in my head. Which means I'm pretty much the best intelligence the brotherhood now has as to the location of the fuerie. And that makes me very useful indeed.

I know Mal's decision to keep me alive didn't hinge on that parlor trick, but I can't deny that it rankles when he says it that way. From Asher, I expect cold calculation. From Mal, I just want love.

Which is why I sound a bit prissy when I say, "So?"

But he just looks at me. And then he repeats, "Tell me what you need. Show me that you trust me, and just tell me."

I sigh. Because he is right. I do need something from him. For that matter, I've probably even made a face a time or two. "All right," I say. "If it comes to it, I need to know that you will stop trying to save me and just kill me."

I am sitting cross-legged, and my knee rests on his thigh. I feel him tense in response to my words, but he says nothing.

I take a breath and continue. "We were lucky in the warehouse. Damn lucky. But it would have been better if you'd slit my throat or put a bullet through my brain."

"Better?" he asks, echoing my word.

"Less risky," I amend.

"The thought didn't even occur to me." From the tone of his voice, I can tell that it horrifies him now.

"I know." I force a smile, trying to lighten the moment. "For thousands of years, that was your mission. Find me. Kill me. How quickly you forget." I broaden the smile. "No wonder Mata Hari was such an excellent spy. A little sex and a man is completely distracted."

I expect a reaction, though I know that laughter might be too much to hope for. But instead, I get nothing. No reply. No reaction. No emotion.

I press my hand against his leg, suddenly needing to reassure him. "I've disturbed you."

"Yes." He reaches down to take my hand, then pulls me to him. I curl against him, my thigh over his and my head tucked against his chest. "I don't like having the truth shoved in my face when I've been trying to avoid it."

I stiffen, his words surprising me. "Then you know I'm right?"

"You're right." He doesn't sound pleased about it. I can't say that I'm crazy about it either.

"So what are we going to do?"

"Exactly what I've been telling you. We get

the weapon out of you. We save the world."

"And if—"

"No." He presses a finger to my lips then shakes his head. "Tomorrow you can tell me your fears. Tonight, you believe my promises."

And as he bends to kiss me, I think that is a deal that I can live with.

CHAPTER 3

I'VE NEVER BEEN one for yoga, but the lotus position seemed like a good choice for trying to get in touch with my inner map.

My eyes are closed. My wrists loose against my knees. I am not saying *ohm*, but if I don't see something soon, I am willing to try that, too.

I've been sitting like this, listening to an album of rainforest sounds that I downloaded, for over thirty minutes. I feel like I'm close . . . and yet nothing has happened other than me getting bone-deep tired.

Thinking—*focusing*—is hard work.

I hear Mal's footsteps, and welcome the excuse to take a break. "How was the meeting?"

"Productive. Phoenix Security has been hired

to provide additional security to a number of high level government officials during an upcoming tour of the southern states."

"That should provide some good intel." Since I'd been off being either dead or someone else during the last few millennia, I was neither part of the creation of Phoenix Security, nor did I know anything about it until recently. But ever since Liam, the co-leader of the brotherhood with Mal, described it to me, I've been asking questions and studying up. Or, at least, I have in my spare time. When I'm not being kidnapped and used as kindling.

Basically, Phoenix Security is a legitimate business that provides high-level security and intelligence services on a global scale. The company provides a sort of rope through the years—an entity that is entitled to be immortal since it isn't actually alive. Brotherhood members can come and go over the decades, changing locations to keep human neighbors from being suspicious of businessmen and women who don't age.

More important, though, Phoenix provides

an excellent source of intel. The brotherhood's primary mission is to find and destroy the fuerie, and the company provides a perch from which to look out across the world.

Now, though, they have me. And if I can get my inner map to kick into high gear, I can provide pinpoint data on the fuerie.

At the moment, though, confidence is low.

"No luck?" Mal asks, moving to sit in the chair nearest me.

I shake my head. "I'm starting to get worried," I admit. "The first time it happened, the image was crystal clear. Ever since then, it's been hazy, even though I've been trying to find clarity. But today, I can't seem to get anything at all. What if I was wrong and this ability isn't going to stick around?"

The map had manifested one night after the weapon had almost gotten out of control. Arguably, I could recreate the circumstances, but that would be far too dangerous, especially as it had taken all of Mal's efforts to pull it back that night.

"Does it feel like you've lost it?" Mal asks,

moving to the floor to sit in front of me.

"That's what's so frustrating," I tell him. "I feel like it's right there—the way you do when you've lost someone's name, but you're certain that you know it. But I just can't seem to bring it up." I let my head fall back. "Honestly, I've been working on it for almost an hour. I had no idea that doing nothing but concentrating could be so exhausting."

"Let me help."

"Yeah?"

He doesn't answer, just slides his hands under mine so that his palms are cupping my knees and the backs of our hands are touching. At first, I feel nothing. Then a slow tingle begins in my hands, like a pinched nerve coming back to life. It spreads, flowing through me like a sparkling web, and I close my eyes and soak up the energy that Mal is giving to me, this gift that I hope will help me see.

At first there is nothing but gleaming colors that I know come from the energy that Mal is pushing into me. But soon I realize that I'm able to focus. That the sparks and colors are power—

a force I can use to draw forth the map. To paint it in my mind's eye.

And though I do not understand how I know this, I realize what it is that I must do in order to make the map appear. After so many thousands of years in the proximity of the weapon that is the source of this power, I have to assume that some part of me has figured this out.

I breathe and focus, breathe and focus, and soon I see it. A map, spread out in front of me, filling the space inside my head.

I open my eyes, and the map seems to fill the world. I stand, and realize that I'm inside it, like standing in the center of a glass globe. It is lit up, sparkling like a Christmas tree, with random dots here and there.

I turn in a slow circle, taking it all in. "There are hundreds of them." My voice is low. I am in awe of this power that I am generating. "They're scattered all over, but there are two solid clusters that I'm betting are more than ten fuerie all holed up in one location."

I'm not terribly good at geography, but I guess that they are in Chicago and Germany, and when I turn to Mal I say only one word. "Atlas."

He doesn't hesitate, but disappears into his office and is back in seconds. The map is starting to fade, but if I concentrate I can still make it out, though it is dim on the walls of this well-appointed room.

I flip through the atlas, comparing the dots I see with the lines and names on the map. "Chicago," I confirm. "And the other cell is in Berlin."

"Are you sure?" he asks, and I shift my focus back to the map. But it is gone now, just that small break in attention enough to send it shimmering away.

"I'm sure," I say.

"Then we don't need to waste time talking about it. Come on."

Mal's brownstone is connected by a small courtyard to 36 East 63rd Street, the location of Dark Pleasures, the members-only club that the brotherhood established years ago. Though only Raine and Callie live full time in the penthouse apartment of the five-story building, most of the members of the brotherhood can be found there, either in Dark Pleasures' VIP room or in one of the offices that are located on the other floors and which the brotherhood uses as the headquarters for Phoenix Security.

We check the VIP room first and find Dagny sitting at one of the tables eating a club sandwich and listening to Raine, who is waving his own sandwich through the air as he illustrates a story.

"Chicago and Berlin," Mal says without preamble.

Dagny puts a hand over her mouth as she swallows, but Raine drops his sandwich onto his plate, shifting immediately into work mode. "Fuerie?"

"A cell, Christina thinks. At least ten."

Raine looks at me, and I nod. "A clearer image than last time, too," I say. "At least, once Mal helped me focus."

"Do you know where in Chicago?" Dagny asks.

I have to shake my head. "Near downtown, I think, but I still have to figure out how to pinpoint."

"What about the amulet?" Dagny asks, referring to the last of seven amulets that, together, have the power to draw the weapon out of me and bind it.

"Not even a hint," I admit. I'd been hoping to see a flash of it, but for some reason the amulet is harder for me to see on the map than the fuerie are. But I know that it is possible, and I hope that with patience and practice I'll be able to find the thing. And the sooner the better.

"That's okay. We can work with this. One of the guys who used to be on my LA team is like Dante. He transferred to Chicago when he hit the mandatory twelve-year move date. We can use him to try to narrow the scope."

The mandatory move date is the date that each member of the brotherhood changes offices in an effort to hide their immortal nature. As for Dante, he has the ability to tell if fuerie are near. Unlike me, though, his range is limited to a few miles.

"Won't that be tedious?" I ask.

"Part of the job," she says. "I'm on it."

She nods to us and leaves, and Mal focuses on Raine. "We don't have a seer on the German team right now. Can you get Dante briefed and on the first plane out of here?"

"Already on it," he says, holding up his phone that clearly displays a text for Dante to get his ass to the club ASAP. "In the meantime, I'll call Brian in Munich. See if there's any intel to narrow the location."

He nods at Mal, then hurries off, presumably to head back to his apartment and get on his computer.

I stand, then swipe my hands together as a cook might brush off flour. "Well, my work here is done."

"Not quite," Mal says, hooking his arm around my waist and pulling me close. I melt immediately, as I always do at his touch.

"No fair," I say, pushing away with a laugh as he brushes his lips over mine. "You're going to distract me."

"Lover, I intend to spend the rest of the day distracting you."

"Mmm. That sounds very tempting." I hook my arms around his neck and press my body against his. I brush my lips over his neck, then laugh when he growls in response. "But," I continue lightly, "I have to get dressed."

He looks down at the maxi style sundress I'd tossed on before going to the VIP room, in deference to Dark Pleasures' dress code, which doesn't run to yoga pants. "I was thinking more along the lines of getting *un*dressed."

"Jeans," I say. "A dress at rehearsal is impractical." I want the freedom to sit on the stage and move around if Eric, the director, wants to engage in various acting exercises.

I watch Mal's face, and I know what he is going to say even before he says it. "You're not going to rehearsal."

"You're right," I say in an overly cheery conversational tone. "I'm going to Bray's, too. I want to pick up some more of my stuff and tell Bray that I'm staying here indefinitely."

After our big showdown with the weapon two days ago, Dagny had brought me a suitcase full of my clothes from my roommate Brayden's apartment. Technically, he's no longer roommate, but we haven't had that official conversation yet, and most of my stuff is in his luxury apartment.

"You can invite Brayden over for that conversation, and he can bring another suitcase of your things with him. And as for rehearsal, you don't need to go. Not today."

"Actually, yeah, I do." I start to head for the exit. "This is Eric's first day back. I want to hear about his LA trip, but more than that, this role is important to me. How does it look when Juliet doesn't show up for rehearsals of *Romeo & Juliet?*"

"From my perspective, it looks like she's trying to stay alive."

I'm in the lobby now, and Mal is beside me. He quickens his pace, then opens the door to the courtyard for me. I foolishly think that this means that I've won the battle, but when he takes my elbow and tugs me to a stop in between Number 36 and his brownstone, I know that nothing is yet resolved.

My shoulders stiffen with frustration. At him, yes, but mostly at my whole situation. "You said the other day that you don't want to change me."

"I don't. But I also said I want to save you.

You can be an actress, Christina. You can be whatever you want. But right now, what you need to be is smart. You're a walking target. Or had you forgotten?"

"Theoretically, I could be a target for decades." I don't say centuries, and from the way he flinches, I know he understands why. Because if Mal doesn't kill me and the fuerie don't capture me and we don't get the weapon out of me, then I am going to grow old. And then, unlike Mal, I will die.

And that, at least, will solve the problem of the weapon until I am reborn again.

He sighs and draws his fingers through his hair. This isn't a position he wants to be in, not a conversation he wants to be having. He's worried, and I get that. But I'm used to making my own decisions, and I came to New York to be an actress, not the focal point for world destruction.

"I want this, Mal," I say softly. "More than that, I need it. I have to be something more than walking dynamite."

His face remains totally expressionless as he

considers my words. It's one of the reasons he's such a good leader—he can consider all sides without anyone on his team knowing what he is thinking until the decision is made.

"Next week," he says. "Tell Eric you're sick. That's just a few days," he adds to ward off my protests. "And in the meantime, we can practice control."

"Not that I don't really love our practice sessions, but didn't we already establish that all the control in the world wouldn't have helped me?"

"When you're tied to a pole and drugged, no. But if you're attacked walking down the street? You need the control so that you can gather yourself and get away safely."

He's not wrong. But even so...

"There are no fuerie nearby," I say. "When I looked at the map, Manhattan was clear."

He tilts his head as he meets my eyes. "Do you remember who kidnapped you?"

I do. Humans. Because not all evil is supernatural.

"That's true," I admit as I hook my arm

through his. "But when they attacked me, I was alone." I rise up on my toes and kiss him on the cheek. "If I'm going to live, Mal, I want to feel alive. So I guess that means you're coming to rehearsal with me."

CHAPTER 4

B EING BACK AT rehearsal feels wonderful. It's nice to play a role other than the Amazing Weapon Woman, and as I stand on stage facing Greg, the sweet-faced man who plays Romeo, I can't help the melancholy that washes over me. Because I want *this* to be my normal. A life with Malcolm. A career on the stage.

I think about my mother, who despite her literal insanity managed to get one thing right: I'm not normal. There's something dark in me. And until we get it out, I will spend my life looking over my shoulder and fearing my own emotions.

In front of me, Greg clears his throat, and I

realize that everyone is waiting on me.

"O think'st though we shall ever meet again?" I ask, my mood adding meaning to the words.

"I doubt it not," he replies. "And all these woes shall serve for sweet discourses in our time to come."

I feel tears well in my eyes. Eric sees them and smiles like a proud director who has coached an actor to an Oscar, and I have to look away. Because there was more truth than acting in my words. All I could think of as we rehearsed the speech was the hundreds of times that Mal and I had been parted by death. And that instead of sweet discourses, we'd shared only worry and fear.

I tell Mal as much when rehearsal is over. "Maybe Romeo is right," he says gently. "Already it's better, isn't it?"

I think about the weapon and how little power I have to fight it. About the fact that if they capture and torture me again, it's a good bet that I'll end up destroying the world. "How the hell is it better?"

"We have each other now," he says, and my heart swells with his words. He leans in to kiss me, not caring that everyone else in the company is staring. Honestly, I don't much care either.

"Yeah," I say, feeling warm and fuzzy and, yes, better. "That is definitely the good part. And once we find the amulet and get this thing out of me, then we can lounge around all day, sharing sweet discourses about our tortured past."

"I can think of things I'd rather share."

"I bet you can. Why don't we go get my stuff, get home, and you can show me what you're thinking?"

"An excellent plan."

Dennis, the brotherhood's driver, had brought us to the theater, but Mal told him not to wait. Rather than call him back now, we take a cab to Bray's luxury high-rise apartment.

Although Brayden is engrossed in med school and fully intends to be a surgeon, he is also the heir apparent to the Kline family fortune, which includes the world-renowned chain of Kline hotels. As far as I'm concerned, he's just Brayden, my best friend since childhood. But the hotel and money connection means that when he offered me a place to stay in New York, I was suddenly exempt from the typical actress angst of a one bedroom, roach-infested apartment shared with six other girls. And that was just fine by me.

I may want the New York acting experience, but I'm happy to leave that aspect of the cliché behind.

Mal and I greet the doorman, then take the elevator up to Brayden's well-appointed apartment. I let myself in, then immediately freeze. The apartment is huge, but open and light-filled. When you enter, the door opens directly into the living area, beyond which is the kitchen, separated only by a half-wall.

All of which means that I have a dead-on view of Brayden on the couch in a very enthusiastic lip lock with Dagny.

Neither seem aware that we are in the room. I glance at Mal, unsure of the etiquette. He looks amused, and clears his throat. Loudly.

They both jump a mile.

"Mal!" Dagny says as she leaps off the couch

to stand at almost military-like attention.

Bray stays on the couch, then grins at me. "Hey, Jay."

"I take it everything's under control in Berlin and Chicago?" Mal asks.

Dagny blushes, but nods. "Wheels are in motion and I should hear back from the team leaders soon. But if the intel was good," she adds, deliberately not looking in my direction, "I expect to hear that it was a success."

If Bray thinks this conversation is odd, he doesn't show it, and I realize that Dagny must have told him that she works for Phoenix Security. Which is true. Just not entirely true.

"We just came by so I could get a few more things. But I forgot to bring my duffel back." I glance at Bray. "Have you got one?"

"No problem." He leads me into the back of the apartment, and I'm grateful when Mal and Dagny don't follow. Right now, I want Bray to myself. Because this moment is bittersweet. I'd come to New York to be his roommate, but I'd managed that for less than a week. Now I'm moving out, and it feels like moving on, and I don't want to leave my best friend behind.

But how can I not? I've always told my secrets to Bray. But this time, those secrets aren't just about me, but about Mal, about Dagny, about the entire brotherhood. And the decision to tell him is not mine to make.

"Hey," he says softly. "You okay?"

"Yeah. Absolutely." I think of Mal, and my smile is one-hundred percent genuine. "Everything is great with Mal."

"Moving fast. Especially for you."

I lift a shoulder. "Maybe I never got close to a guy before because I hadn't found the right guy."

I expect Brayden, who goes through women like most people go through soft drinks, to scoff. Instead he nods thoughtfully. "Yeah. The right person can change everything."

I raise my brows. "Is that so?"

He holds up his hands. "Just making conversation."

"Sure. Right." I can hear the laughter in my voice, and it matches the smile on his face.

For a moment, I pack in silence, emptying

drawers that I'd only recently filled into the duffel bag that he pulled out from under the bed.

"Listen," he finally says. "Mal seems like a great guy, and Dagny thinks the world of him. But if things don't work out, you know you can come back, right?"

"I know. But things have already worked out." Since I can't tell Bray that I've actually been with Mal for several thousand years, I don't elaborate. Instead, I tease him. "Besides, are you sure? From what I've seen, my bedroom might be occupied."

"Trust me, Jay," he says with a very smug smile, "your bedroom isn't going to be used at all."

When the duffel is full, we go back out to find Mal and Dagny at the small bar that serves as a breakfast area, both with a glass of wine. I hide my smile, but I'm glad to see that Dagny feels at home here. I like her, and I love Brayden. And even though I know it would be crazy insane for Bray to get involved with an immortal woman, it's clear they make each other happy. And at the moment, I think that's the most important thing of all.

"I need to get back," Dagny tells Bray. "I'd like to be at my computer when my teams report in. But why don't you come? We could all have some dinner in the lounge?"

She means the VIP lounge, of course, where non-members are really not allowed. Especially non-members who don't know the truth.

I see the hesitation on Mal's face, but it fades when he looks at both me and Dagny. It's clear we both want Bray there, and so he nods. "Sounds great. I could use a steak tonight."

"Thank you," I whisper as I take his hand and head for the door.

"It's just dinner."

"It's more than that." I pause and look up at him. "You make me happy, Mal. And considering all the crap that's going on around me, I think that's a pretty big thing." I shrug, feeling suddenly foolish and sentimental.

But if my sentimentality bothers Mal, he doesn't show it. Instead, he brushes my lower lip with his thumb, then bends down to kiss me softly. "You make me happy, too," he says, with so much tenderness in his voice that my eyes fill with tears despite my smile going wide.

I'm still smiling when we hit the sidewalk.

Mal pulls out his phone. "Let me text Dennis."

"It's less than five blocks," Bray says.

Mal hesitates, looks at me.

"It's a gorgeous night," I say.

He waits a beat, then nods. "Fine. We walk."

It really is a gorgeous night, warm without being humid, and no moon in the sky. The ambient light blocks most of the stars, but the city still looks like a glowing angel, asleep under a blanket of velvet.

I have my head tilted back, looking at the silhouette of the buildings against the night sky, when the gang of six surrounds us. Three in the front and three in the back.

And, yes, they have faces of flame.

The fuerie.

I want to scream. To shout that they aren't supposed to be on the island. But not only is that stupid, I have no time. Because even though only seconds have passed, one of them has grabbed me, and is holding me tight.

I feel my pulse kick up. The fear rising inside me. "Mal!" I call his name, but it doesn't matter. He's already in the fight—already moving fast. Already doing what needs to be done to save me.

Behind him, Dagny has her fire sword extended, and she whips it around, managing to behead two of them as Brayden stumbles backward, obviously weak at the knees. She stabs them quickly through the heart, and they turn to dust.

Stupidly, I think that is a good thing. Because though this block is empty right now, any moment some unsuspecting New Yorker might walk up. And what would they think if they saw a headless body?

The thought makes me giggle, and from somewhere deep inside I know that is a wildly inappropriate response and that I am in shock.

Bray's pain-filled scream restores my focus, and I cry out in horror as he falls, his chest bleeding where a fuerie's whip has sliced him open.

No. No, no, no!

I'm angry and scared, and as the fuerie tightens his grip on my arm—as Mal slashes down three more of the fuerie in a frenzy of sword and motion—I try desperately to keep control. I'm breathing deep. I'm fighting. And I'm managing—I am—but then something hot and hard jabs into my lower back.

I cry out in pain. Blinding, horrific, mind-filling pain.

And the weapon rises more.

"Enough!" Mal cries, and as he does, he lifts his hand, and I feel myself and the fuerie being thrown backward, pushed through the air by the force of Mal's will.

We slam against a wall, then collapse on the ground, the fuerie's grip on me weakened.

I roll to the side, ignoring the pain in my lower back, and in that moment, Mal leaps forward and jabs his fire sword through the fuerie's heart.

In seconds, there is only a pile of dust beside me.

Mal bends down in front of me and takes my hands. "Pull it back," he says. "You're safe.

You're good. They didn't cut you; they burned you. It's just pain, and it will fade, and Jessica can heal the scar. Breathe with me now. Come on, back it off."

His words are comforting, and I breathe slowly, forcing my body to relax. Easing the weapon down. Saving myself. Saving the world.

"I'm okay," I finally say. My voice sounds thin, but strong.

Mal looks at me a moment, as if assessing the truth of my statement. Then he stands and looks behind him.

Dagny is squatting beside Brayden, and I'm happy to see that the wound is not deep. I can see the confusion on his face, along with a fear that is tempered only by Dagny's gentle presence beside him.

Mal takes a step their direction, and as he does, Dagny rises and steps in front of Bray. She and I both know what Mal intends—he's going to take Bray's memories.

"No," she says, even as I say the same word at the same time.

Mal looks between the two of us.

"Please," I say. "Please, Mal. Don't."

Dagny says nothing, perhaps assuming that my plea will be sufficient. I hope she's right.

After a moment, Mal nods, then walks back to me and helps me to my feet. A few yards away, Dagny does the same, helping Bray stand even as the limo pulls up. I hadn't noticed, but Dagny or Mal must have summoned it.

As we move to the car, Brayden winces. Then he catches my eyes.

Finally, he just exhales. "So is anyone going to tell me what the fucking hell just happened? Or am I just going to have to guess?"

CHAPTER 5

"**B**ETTER?" JESSICA ASKS me. Her long hair is swept back into a ponytail and she wears no makeup. Even so, she is stunning. But it's not her looks that you notice first about Jessica—it's her presence. She's a healer—the brotherhood's primary doctor—and she has a confidence coupled with humor that would put even the most jaded human at ease.

I adored her the moment I met her, and now that she's ensured that the burn on my back no longer pounds with agonizing pain, I think I've developed a little bit of a girl crush.

"Is there a scar?" I ask, twisting as I try to look over my shoulder and see the injury site.

"Oh, please. You come to me for treatment

and then insult me?"

I laugh. "Fair enough. Thanks." I glance across the room to where Bray is stretched out on a couch, completely dead to the world. We're in the guest suite of Number 36, where Jessica had treated me for injuries before. She has since told me that she has an official triage station in the building, but that she prefers to work here since the atmosphere is more calming.

"He's okay, right?" Brayden had passed out in the limo, but whether from the injury or from the general weirdness of the situation, I don't know.

"He's fine. And this makes it easy. I want him to sleep, and now I don't have to call in Mal to take some of his energy, or rely on a dose of narcotics."

Mal isn't in the room. He'd kissed me hard, then left me in Jessica's care so that he could go brief the others on the furies' arrival on the island of Manhattan.

I know that I didn't misread the map, but I still feel foolish. Considering rehearsal and the time at Bray's, several hours had passed since I'd taken a look. And the fuerie are as likely to drive, fly, or take the train into the city as anyone else.

On the couch, Bray stirs. Immediately, I hop off the table I'd been sitting on and go to his side.

"Hey, you're going to be fine."

"Hurts like a bitch," he mumbles.

"I know," I say truthfully. I'd suffered essentially the same injury not too long ago—and almost destroyed the world from the pain.

"What happened?" He presses his fingers to the bridge of his nose. "Had the weirdest dream."

"It's going to be better soon," I say, then scoot to one side so that Jessica can get to his chest. She gently peels his tattered shirt away, and then I watch, fascinated, as she does to Bray what she'd done to me.

Slowly, she draws her finger over the injury. As she does, the layers of flesh knit back together, so that all is left is a pink scar, looking newly healed. She repeats the process, and this time the scar disappears, leaving perfect flesh.

I exhale, relieved. I didn't like the idea of

Bray being permanently scarred because of me.

During Jessica's treatment, I'd been watching her heal the wound. Now I shift my attention to Bray, who looks completely perplexed.

"It's okay," Dagny says, coming up and putting a hand on his shoulder. "You're all fixed up now."

He says nothing, just shifts on the couch, his intelligent eyes taking everything in. His ripped shirt and unmarred skin. Me. Jessica. Dagny. And now Mal is entering the suite with Raine at his side, Raine's sleeves of tats revealed by the T-shirt he wears.

"I'm going out on a limb and saying that you people aren't from around here." Bray looks at me. "What's going on, Jay?"

"Bray—" I cut myself off, unsure what to say.

"We'll explain everything," Dagny promises. She leans over to kiss his forehead as I squeeze his hand, both in support and in apology.

"You need to rest," Mal says, stepping in beside me.

"The hell I do. What I need are answers."

"Soon," Mal promises, then touches his forehead. "Take a nap, Bray," he orders. "We'll talk later."

And as I watch, Bray's eyes close and he drifts off into slumber.

"Just sleep, right?" I demand. "He'll remember?"

"He'll remember," Mal says. "But I meant what I said. He needs to rest. And Dagny has work. And you and I need to talk."

He is tense. His voice tight, almost rough.

I lick my lips and meet Dagny's eyes. She gives me a small smile as if in solidarity. We both know that Mal isn't happy. We shouldn't have been out there. We shouldn't have been ambushed.

And maybe I shouldn't have gone to rehearsal in the first place.

Fuck.

I stand, because I know there is no way to avoid this. Because right now I'm feeling pretty damn guilty anyway. I'd known an attack was a possibility, but I'd discounted it because I wanted my life to be normal. Because I didn't want to deal with the reality that lives inside me.

And Bray was the one who paid the price.

Thank God he hadn't paid in full, because while Jessica can heal, she can't restore the dead. And if the fuerie's whip had taken Bray from me, I don't know that I could have survived the pain and the guilt.

Considering the weapon that lives inside me, I'm not sure the world could have survived, either.

MAL PACED THE length of his den on the second floor of his home. For the last hour, he'd held everything in, fighting back emotion so that he could be calm and controlled. So that he could brief the team about the attack. So that he could make sure Bray was taken care of. So that he could double-check that the security at both Number 36 and here at his brownstone was up to par and locked down.

Now, though, everything was churning inside him, and he knew damn well that the wild mire of fear and anger and frustration would spew out with only the slightest provocation.

"Mal?" Christina's soft voice drifted over from where she stood at the top of the stairs. It filtered through the red haze in his mind, and that was it. That was the trigger. He reached down, scooped up the nearest thing he saw, and hurled it across the room.

It was a small pottery bowl that he'd picked up at some street fair somewhere, and the sound that it made when it shattered against the wall was almost satisfying. Shards of clay clattered to the polished wooden floor, and Mal was left staring at a bowl-sized indentation in the wall.

She was at his side in an instant, her arms sliding around his waist as she pressed her body against his back. Immediately, he felt calmer. Just her touch alone was like a balm.

"I'm sorry," she whispered. "It's all my fault, and I'm so, so sorry."

He closed his eyes in defense against the pain he heard in her voice. "No. This wasn't all your fault. I fucked up, Christina." He pulled out of her embrace so that he could turn to face her. "I wanted to see you happy. And I let you talk me into doing something I damn well knew was a risk."

Her smile wavered. "Like I said. It's all my fault."

"No," he repeated. "I have responsibilities. A mission. A goddamn duty to protect the brotherhood. To fight the fuerie. To keep my people safe. To keep *you* safe. I'm in charge of a team," he said. "And tonight I let all of that slide—every bit of it—because I looked at you and wanted to let you keep some piece of the life you still have. I had a duty to look after the team," he continued. "And I breached that duty.

"So, no, it wasn't all your fault." He looked at her, speaking gently. "But you do share some of the blame. You're part of the brotherhood, Christina. I need you to be part of the team."

"I am," she said. But she didn't meet his eyes.

"No, lover, you're not." He stroked her hair, twirling a soft lock around his finger. He wanted to bend over her and bury his face in her hair. To breathe in the clean fresh scent of her. To get lost in the thrill of touching her, seeing her, smelling her.

But this wasn't the time. They needed to do this; they needed to resolve this. "Talk to me, Christina."

He watched as her shoulders rose and fell, and his heart twisted when she looked at him with tears glistening in her eyes. "I am part of the team," she said firmly. "And at the same time, I'm not." She pulled away from him, then went to sit on the couch. Her feet were bare, and she pulled them up onto the cushion so that she was hugging her knees to her chest.

"I love you, Mal. You have to know that. But at the same time, I can't help but feel like Christina is just a role that I'm playing. *You* feel real to me. But this life doesn't. Even though I know that it's as real as it gets and there's something horrible and deadly inside me, it still all feels surreal. Does that make sense?"

"It does," he said. And because he wanted her to keep talking, he said no more.

She waited, then cleared her throat to fill the silence. After a moment, though, she continued. "As Jaynie, I never really got close to anyone.

And I was never much of a team player. You know that."

"Yes."

"And you said we could take it slow." Her words were a plea, and he went to her, then sat beside her on the couch and took one of her hands in his.

"I did," he said. "But I meant us. You and me. And I'll hold fast to that promise. I love you, Jaynie Christina, and we have all the time in the world to get to know each other again, wholly and completely. But where the brotherhood is concerned, we don't have that luxury. I need everyone to be part of the team, part of the unit. It's a matter of survival. And if I can't keep you alive, then I can't love you forever. And that's just not acceptable to me."

"I don't like it much either," she said, sniffling a little as she wiped away a tear. "I know it would be easier if I'd just fallen back into Christina once my memories came back. But there's too much of Jaynie mixed up in me now. Too much of everyone else I've ever been." She sucked in a shaky breath. "And I am sorry for that, Mal. I'm sorry I'm not the woman you loved anymore."

Is that what she thought? Good god, how could she possibly believe that?

He clutched her hand and waited until she was looking straight at him before he spoke. "We've both changed, lover. How could we not after so much time? And I'll grant you that your change was more violent than mine. New lives. New experiences. And all tangled up inside you like so much noise. So you're right—you're not the woman I loved. But I'm not the same man either. How could I be? How could either of us be anything other than the people that time has made us? And do you know what I see when I look at you now? I see a woman who is smart and funny and full of life. She's loyal and she's fearless. And even though she damn well better not do it again, I love the fact that she defies me."

At that, she laughed, and Mal relaxed just a little.

"I love that she fights my decisions and makes her own. That she sees what she wants, and she goes after it. Don't you see, lover? You aren't the woman I loved anymore. But you are the woman I love."

He kissed her then, so gently his lips barely touched her skin, but even so, sparks of awareness shot through him. "I hope that you love the man I've become, but right now, I only need to know that you trust me. As your mate. As your leader. Because if you don't trust me, I can't protect you. And I can't lose you again. I might be immortal, but that is something I simply couldn't survive."

She blinked, and a tear trickled slowly down her cheek as she nodded. "I do trust you," she said as she moved to straddle his lap. She pressed her palm to his cheek, and when he looked at her face—at the heat building in her eyes—he knew that she was telling the truth.

With a mischievous smile, she wiggled a bit on his lap, and his cock immediately went hard. She slid her hand between their bodies and stroked him, then leaned forward so her mouth was close to his ear. "I screwed up, Mal. What do you do when one of your team screws up?"

"Depends on the screw up." He practically growled the words, because as far as he was concerned the time for conversation was over.

"Bad." Her voice was low and sultry, and her breath was ragged. "Really bad." She pulled back a bit so that he could see her face. There was heat rising in her eyes, but he thought that he also saw a hint of insecurity, and he couldn't help but wonder at it.

"You might impose some sort of disciplinary action, right?" she asked.

He couldn't help his smile of understanding. "Actually, lover," he said as heat and need ricocheted through him. "I just might."

MY BREATH CATCHES in my throat. "Yeah? What are you going to do?" I press a kiss to his jaw. "Ground me?" Another to his neck. "Cut off my allowance?" Lower still to his chest, my lips against his T-shirt. "Send me to my room without supper?"

"All very interesting ideas." Mal's voice is low

and sultry as it curls through me, igniting every cell in my body. "But I want to hear it from you. What punishment do you think is appropriate?"

I lick my lips. "I screwed up." My voice is low. Barely a whisper. "I really did. So I think you should probably spank me."

"Do you?" I hear the way his voice rises in both interest and decadent promise.

I incline my head. "Yes." The word is like a trigger, making my body soft. Making me wet.

His hands slide over my back, then down to cup my ass. With one harsh motion he pulls me tighter against him, our hips grinding together, his erection rubbing against my crotch. And all I can think is that I want to be naked. That I want us both to strip off these jeans, because I need to feel skin on skin. Right then, I think I need that as much as I need to breathe.

"Please," I say. And though I have been shy before, that hesitancy has slipped away. I want this. More than that, I need it. And I think that Mal does, too.

He bends forward, his cheek brushing mine as he presses his mouth to my ear. I shiver from the contact. From the way his beard stubble scratches my tender skin. The way his tongue softly teases the edge of my ear. "I can't tell you how hard the thought of my palm against your bare ass makes me," he says, his words making my body clench in anticipation. "But no. I'm not going to punish you."

"Oh." I sit back, embarrassed, my posture going stiff. I start to slide off of him, but he presses one hand against my thigh to hold me in place.

"This isn't about punishment, lover, it's about trust. It's about me knowing that you trust me enough to hand me control. And it's about you trusting me not to push you too far."

He holds my chin as he looks at me. But though his touch is gentle, I see the flare of heat on his face. "Do you understand?"

I nod. My entire body seems hyperaware. His touch. His scent. I'm aware of my breathing, my heartbeat. Even the tiny hairs on the back of my neck tingle with anticipation of his touch.

"Stand up."

I do, but I feel suddenly awkward and have

to fight the urge to cross my arms over my chest. "Mal."

He leans back on the couch, looking completely relaxed. One eyebrow cocks up. "Yes?"

I shake my head. "I don't know," I say. "I think I just wanted to hear your name."

His smile is slow and very, very sexy. For a long moment he says nothing, just looks at me, his gaze starting at my feet and traveling up until our eyes meet. I take a step toward him without even thinking, as if there is an invisible string between us and he is slowly—very slowly— reeling me in.

"Take off your clothes."

His words stop me. "What?"

"You heard me."

I drag my teeth over my lower lip. Apparently we're playing games. But that's okay with me. Because if we're playing a game, then I'm going to play to win. Although I have a feeling that with this kind of game, even the loser wins a prize.

"Now," he says, and I lift my chin in response.

"Yes, sir." I flash him what I hope looks like an innocent smile, then take the hem of my T-shirt and pull it over my head. I let it fall to the floor, leaving me clad only in my pink lace bra.

The jeans have a button-fly, and I keep my eyes fixed on Mal's as I very slowly and methodically unfasten each button. I take a step closer to him, then hook my fingers in the belt loops and start to tug the denim over my hips. "Want to do the honors?"

I think I see temptation in his eyes, but he just shakes his head. One small, firm motion. "I think I'll just enjoy the view."

"Suit yourself," I say, then ease the jeans down until they are pooled around my ankles. I've already taken off my shoes, so I step out, leaving me in only the pink bra and equally pink boy shorts style underwear.

I stand for a moment, watching him as intently as he is watching me. I feel hot. Needy. And as his eyes travel deliberately over all of me, I have to bite my lip in defense against the urge to slide my hand between my legs and touch myself.

"Do it."

My eyes flutter open—I didn't realize I'd closed them. "What?"

I'd heard him perfectly clearly, of course, but the command—issued with such power and heat—has cut through me in a way that has my sex clenching and my nipples hardening almost painfully against the lace of my bra. I want to comply, but god help me, I want to hear him say it again.

"You want to touch yourself," he says. He spreads his arms along the back of the couch. Except for the erection straining against his jeans, he looks completely relaxed and casual. "I want to watch. So do it."

"Mal…"

But he just shakes his head.

I swallow, but then I close my eyes and press my palm flat against my belly. I slide my hand down under the waistband of my underwear until I'm stroking my sex. I'm hot and wet, and I gasp from the delicious sensation. But it isn't my touch that I want. "Please," I whisper. "Mal, please."

"Come here," he says, and I almost melt with relief.

I go to him and stand in front of the couch between his legs. He tugs the underwear down, then nods at me, indicating that I should step free. Then he sits up straight and draws his legs together, tilting his finger as he does. I know what that means. I'm supposed to bend over his knee.

I hesitate, then draw my teeth over my lower lip. I'm nervous, yes, but I'm also desperately turned on. And so I comply, bending across his lap so that my ass is right there in front of him and his erection is pressed against my abdomen. And in that moment, I know that this is right— this is perfect. Because I am open and exposed, my head down and my body vulnerable. I couldn't survive this—couldn't want this—if I didn't trust him. And I do. So help me, I trust him completely.

"Lovely," he murmurs as he strokes the globe of my rear with the palm of his hand. And when he slides his hand between my legs and slips his fingers inside me, my body trembles with need and a wild desire rises inside me, and I'm suddenly afraid that this is a mistake. Because surely we are playing with fire.

"Mal—" I draw a breath, trying to hold myself together. "We shouldn't—I can't—"

"Yes," he says. "You can. *We* can. Now hush," he adds, and punctuates the order with a firm smack on my rear. I cry out from the sharp pain of impact, then moan a bit as he rubs my rear, soothing the sting even as heat spreads through me. He slips his fingers inside me again and I groan with pleasure, my body clenching tight around him as he draws free. I want to cry out in protest, because despite the fear—despite feeling the weapon rising in conjunction with my pleasure—I want more.

Another smack. And once again he rubs the sting away.

"Again?"

"Yes," I say. "Please, yes." But he just strokes my rear, soft and gentle despite the way I writhe against him in unspoken demand.

"Do you trust me? Will you let me take you as far as you can go, but no farther? Will you do that for me? For us?"

"Yes." I have to force the word out. My throat is too full of desire. My body too flush with need. "Yes. Yes, please."

"Good," he says. "I want that, too." He lands another spank, then another and another. Between each he soothes the sting with the soft stroke of his palm, then teases my clit and fingerfucks me until I am just about to go out of my mind. Which, of course, is the entire point, but that's hard to remember when wild pleasure is spiraling through me, rising up higher and higher and pulling the darkness out with it.

"Mal—oh god, Mal!"

"It's okay," he says. "I've got you." But instead of taking me down, he's still stirring me up. Touching and stroking and teasing me, taking me closer and closer to the edge—

And closer and closer to the end.

I whimper, so close to the edge and so full of the dark that I'm starting to fear that Mal has lost control. That this was a mistake. That we should never have gone this far because there's just no way to come back from this, and we've screwed it all up, and—

No.

Absolutely totally *no.*

I trust him.

I trust him, and we're okay, and I'm fine. And I'm listening to his words. Calming me. Telling me to pull it back. To tamp the weapon down. To breathe, to breathe, to breathe.

And then that's all there is. Just breath and life and light.

The weapon's gone, only smoky tendrils remaining, curling through me as if in dark reminder of what could have been. Of what we fought.

With a shock, I realize that I'm no longer bent over Mal's lap. I'm in his arms, pressed tight against him, and my eyes are closed tight. Slowly, I open them, then manage a wavering smile. "You were right," I say.

"I know." He lowers his head to kiss me, and when he pulls back, I see humor in the gray of his eyes. "And I think you liked it, too."

I don't quite meet his eyes when I say, "Maybe. A little." I peer up at him. "I'll like it more when you can take me all the way, but until then, I have to say this was just fine."

"I told you to trust me," he says with a laugh.

I grin in return. "Yeah," I say. "You definitely did."

CHAPTER 6

"I THINK I deserve some sort of award for not completely flipping out," Bray says.

We're in the VIP lounge, and he and I and Dagny have been sitting at one of the dark corner tables for the last half-hour. Mal is across the room, discussing strategy with Liam, his co-leader of the brotherhood. Asher is there, too. He's the brotherhood's second-in-command. And though he very enthusiastically wanted me dead until just recently, once he learned that I can see the amulet, he conceded that I am more valuable alive.

Good news for me, but I fear what will happen if I don't ever manage to acquire the piece.

It's late afternoon, and they're all three smoking cigars, and though the smoke is filtered out by a state of the art ventilation system, some of the scent remains, filling the air with a woodsy, almost chocolate scent that I can't deny I like.

Raine and Callie are across the room, sitting at one of the smaller tables huddled over a game of chess. I'm terrible at the game, but I've learned that Callie is kick-ass and has given Raine a run for his money several times.

Dante's still in Germany, and I'm not sure where Jessica is.

And although Mal has mentioned another of the brotherhood who is assigned to New York, Trace, I haven't seen him yet. According to Dagny, that's a good thing. Apparently Trace and Raine aren't exactly the best of friends.

Not that I have outlined all of that for Bray. On the contrary, Dagny and I have been taking turns very slowly telling him the basics, both about me and about the brotherhood in general.

And, of course, about the fuerie.

"And you guys are sure that this is all real? I mean, it's quite possible I hit my head really, really hard."

"It's real," I say. "Believe me, I was pretty freaked out myself a few days ago."

"Except you had your memories to back up the story, right? All I have is your word."

I frown. My memories aren't exactly the most reliable. When you grow up with an insane mother, you learn early on to question reality.

Bray, of course, knows all about my mom, and I see him wince as soon as he realizes the import of what he's said. "Sorry, Jay. Of course it would have been weird for you. I wasn't—"

"It's okay," I assure him. I lift a shoulder in a shrug. "And now I know that despite her craziness, my mom got one thing right. There really is something dark and horrible inside me."

He drags his fingers through his hair. "See, I still don't understand that. This weapon is in you, but you can get it out with an amulet?"

"Stones can hold energy," Dagny says. "And these were mined in our dimension, so they are more potent than earth-based gemstones. The combined energy of all seven stones has remarkable power."

"All right," he says. "I get that. I did a paper

in undergrad about the healing power of gemstones. It was pretty interesting stuff, actually, and while I don't intend to put rubies inside my patients when I open them up, I can't deny that in some cases gem-based therapy seemed to have results. But," he continues, leaning forward to put his elbows on the polished wood table, "what I really want to know is this—can I get another drink? And this time, make it a double?"

Dagny laughs, then brushes a kiss over his cheek. "Sure. Just give me a second. I need to tell Mal and Liam a couple of things."

She shoots me a quick glance as she leaves, and I understand the subtext: *You've known him longer; make sure he's really okay.*

"So today I learned my new girlfriend is immortal and my best friend could destroy the world." He frowns, rocking his head a bit as if considering a weighty problem. "Not the best day, but on the whole, I think it ranks better than a med school final exam."

"Thanks," I say.

"For what?"

"For not freaking out."

"Inside I'm a little freaked," he admits. "I'm practicing for when I'm in the operating room. No freak outs allowed in there. I like Jessica, by the way. That's a damn nifty trick she has." He reaches out and takes my hand. "Your trick's a bit dicier. You doing okay?"

"I am," I say. "I've had my moments of serious freakout, but that's kind of the norm for this kind of thing, right?"

"Got news for you, Jay. There is no 'this kind of a thing.'"

On that, I have to agree. "To be honest, everything would be fabulous if it weren't for the weapon. I mean, I'm back with Mal—"

"Which is weird right there. A few days ago you didn't even know him. Now you're attached to him for all eternity."

I nod slowly, trying to gather my thoughts in a way that will help Bray to understand. "It's like I saw him, and that opened a door. And all the old memories and feelings came rushing back. He *is* my husband, mate, soul mate, whatever you want to call it. And I know it and I feel it. But

I'm feeling it as Christina. As Jaynie, I'm still in that wild, passion-filled stage. I know he's the one—I can feel it here," I add, pressing my hand to my heart. "I trust him, Bray. I trust him, and I love him. But it's still a little strange. Because even though I have the memories, it feels like we skipped right over all the romance-filled dating parts."

"But not the sex," he says, deadpan. "Please tell me you didn't skip the sex."

I feel my cheeks go hot as I remember the intensity with which Mal and I made love last night. "Um, no. Definitely not skipping that part."

"So what's his take on it?"

"He's great," I say truthfully. "And patient. He says that we're getting to know each other again. But I know the whole deal is hard for him. I mean, he killed me hundreds of times, and each time all he really wanted was to pull me close. Can you even imagine?"

"No," Bray says. "I really can't. It sounds like the worst kind of hell."

I nod, because I can't either, and I would

give anything if I could erase the pain of Mal's past, and I can only hope that the future that lies before us dulls some of that lingering ache.

"The truth is," I continue, "everything would be amazing if it weren't for the weapon." I suck in air. "I'm so sorry you got hurt, Bray. It's all my fault."

"It's not," he says. We've been down this road already today. Several times, in fact.

I shrug. "Say what you want, I was being foolish and arrogant and careless."

"Sounds like half the people wandering the streets of New York," he retorts, making me laugh. "Seriously, if I'd ended up dead, I'd be pissed. But I'm fine, and we should just move on. Lesson learned."

I nod, but even though I believe him, and even though Mal and I have been over this territory, too, the guilt still lingers. I imagine it always will.

Across the room, I see Dagny looking our way, and I lift my chin to signal that she can return anytime. "I'm glad things are going well with you two."

"So am I," he says. "I like her. The whole immortal thing throws me for a loop, but I figure I'll deal with that later. One step at a time, right?"

That's what my mom's therapist used to say, and although for the most part I thought he was an ass, about that, he may have had the right idea.

"Yeah," I agree. "One step at a time."

As Dagny heads toward us, the door on the far side of the room that connects the VIP area to the members' lounge opens, and Tanya, the receptionist I'd met during my very first visit to Dark Pleasures, pokes her head in. Dagny detours that direction and meets her at the door, then continues toward Bray and me carrying a glass of scotch for Bray and the long white box with a red bow that Tanya has handed her.

"Oooh," I say. "What did you get?"

"You tell me." She pushes the box across the table to me. Sure enough, it's addressed to Jaynie Christina Hart. I look across the room, but Mal is still deep in conversation with Liam, and though I have the odd sensation that he is watching me, I never catch him in the act.

"Open it!" Dagny urges.

Since that seems like a solid plan, I give the ribbon tug and loosen the bow. I pull it free, and then lift the top off the box.

Inside are a dozen perfect red roses. And nestled among the stems is a small card. I take it out and read it, my breath catching as I do. And this time when I look at Mal, he is looking back, and he nods his head almost imperceptibly as if to say, *Yes.*

"Well?" Brayden asks.

When I hold out the card to Bray, I am grinning so wide that it hurts.

Then. Now. Always.
I love you,
Yours eternally,
Mal

I take out the flowers, hold them to my nose and breathe deep. Apparently we're not skimping on the romance after all.

I lift my face and find Mal watching me, his expression so full of love it makes me sigh.

Always, he mouths.

Forever, I reply.

AN HOUR LATER, our table is full to overflowing. I'm on Mal's lap, warm in his arms. Across from us, Dagny sits on the arm of Bray's chair as he holds her around the waist. Callie and Raine are on the small bench that backs up to the wall, and Liam and Jessica have pulled up a chair and are squeezed in between Raine and Bray.

Even Asher has joined us, though he is focusing more on the text messages he is sending back and forth with Dante than our conversation. As far as the conversation goes, it is flowing as free as the scotch. Bray, however, is the only one who seems to be getting tipsy, and when I whisper to Mal that I've had four drinks and am still surprisingly upright, he replies that an inability to get drunk is a side effect of the brotherhood's particular brand of immortality.

"Apparently the weapon didn't steal that from you," he whispers. "As your memories have returned, so has your ability to metabolize alcohol."

Across the table, Bray smacks his hand on the polished wood, yanking my attention from Mal. "So here's the thing I don't get," he mutters, clearly on the downside of drunk. "How can she be a map?" He aims a wobbly finger toward me and almost knocks over Dagny's wine glass in the process. "She's my best friend, and I think I would know if she was a map."

Dagny meets my eyes. "Lightweight," she says, and I laugh.

"I'm serious," Bray says. "I want to see."

Around the table, the others look amused. For her part, Dagny looks mildly embarrassed. "This wasn't how I intended him to meet everybody."

"He's fine," Jessica says. "And loopier than he normally would be. The healing," she says to me as an aside. "It wipes mortals out."

"All the more reason you should do this for the mortal," Bray says. He focuses on me. As much as he can focus, anyway. "Come on, Jay. Parlor trick time."

Despite the fact that I am trying very hard to burrow into Mal, I don't seem to be getting anywhere.

"At the risk of egging him on," Liam finally says, "I think it would be a good idea for you to do a sweep now. We know there were six on the island earlier. Let's see if they brought friends."

"Yes!" Brayden punches the air.

I roll my eyes, but at the same time I push myself up so that I'm sitting straight. "Right here?" I ask, looking between Mal and Liam.

"Can you do it here?"

"I'm not sure I can do it at all," I admit. "Lately it's been hit and miss."

"You can do it," Mal says. He presses his hand to my back and I close my eyes, soaking in his strength. Reminding myself through his touch that he will always be there.

"Okay," I say with a grimace toward Bray. "Here goes nothing."

I lay my hands flat on the table as I lean forward with eyes closed. Mal keeps his hand on me, and I am grateful that he knows with such innate certainty what I need.

I start to breathe, slow and steady, trying to be calm and collected and not force it. Hoping that by sliding out of myself, I'll bring the world into focus around me. And slowly—so slowly—I feel it starting to come together. I'm not sure if it's me or if Mal is feeding me energy, but the truth is that I don't care. We're a team.

We're a couple.

And I both trust him and rely on him.

That simple truth fills me. Hell, it relaxes me. And as my muscles soften and my mind opens, the map spreads out around me, filling my head, taking over my world.

"I see it," I whisper as I open my eyes. As before, the map now seems to be projected on the walls around me. I stand up, feeling a bit like a girl in a dream and turn a slow circle in the tiny space between the table and Mal's chair.

I am searching for the United States. For New York. For Manhattan. Letting my eyes skip over the scatter of lights like fireflies against the night. "So many," I whisper. "But not here."

I hear a vague mumbling, and think that my friends must be talking. But I don't see them. I don't hear them. I see only the map. I feel only the fuerie and—

And?

"None on Manhattan," I say. "But there is something." I move forward, though only in my mind. I hadn't realized I could do this before, but I'm bringing it into focus. Like zooming in on a computer map, making the image bigger and bigger until I am standing on a street. I walk a block, then look around for a street sign.

As I do, I see the building.

That's it.

That's the one.

That's where the amulet is now.

CHAPTER 7

MAL LOOKED INTO her now-clear eyes. Before, she'd been somewhere else. Physically there, but mentally gone. For a moment—one single, horrible moment—he'd been afraid that he'd lost her again. This time not to death, but to the madness that she feared.

That she'd gone into the map in her mind, and had gotten lost there, with no way to find her way back to him.

And now that she was looking at him with triumph, it took every bit of his strength not to pull her into his arms, kiss her hard, and tell her to never, ever leave him again.

Christ, where was his head?

She made him crazy with passion. With worry. With longing.

He wanted to hold her close, and yet he didn't want her to feel trapped.

He wanted her safe.

He wanted this to be over.

That was the bottom line: he simply wanted her. He simply wanted everything.

"So?" Brayden said, even that simple word coming out in a slur. "Did you see the bad guys?"

She turned in another circle, her eyes bright and her smile widening until she found Mal's eyes again. "They're not on the island," she said. "But I saw the amulet."

As if on cue, everyone except Brayden leaned in. "Are you sure?" Liam asked.

"Where?" Mal demanded.

She reached for his hand, and he took it, then pulled her onto his lap. She came easily, and the moment felt warm and comfortable despite the tension in the air and the stirrings of a mission in development. "Nearby," she said, then rattled off the address and the name of a store—Orlov Antiques and Fine Jewelry.

"Oh!" Callie said. "I know that store. Or, at

least, I know of it."

"Could you get us access?" Ash asked.

She shook her head. "Oh, no. When I say I know it, it's because Daddy used to talk about the owner. Not a nice man. Not at all."

"Fuerie?"

Callie's brow furrowed. "I don't think so. I've met him a couple of times, including once after I came back to deal with Daddy's illness. I didn't get a weird vibe and I didn't see the flames on his face."

"That doesn't mean much," Raine said. "You weren't aware of who you were then."

She nods. "That's true. The first time I saw the flames, I was scared and the adrenaline kicked me into gear. Orlov's unpleasant, but I wouldn't call him scary."

"And I didn't see any fuerie around," Christina said. "Though Orlov could just be off the island."

"A minion," Raine said. "A human who's working with the fuerie."

"I bet that's it," Callie said. "Daddy said there were rumors he was tied into the Russian mafia.

And that fits. His security puts Fort Knox to shame. I mean, yes, he has some high end pieces, but I think he was locking up more than estate sale diamonds at night."

Mal leaned back, considering. "What do you mean it put Fort Knox to shame?"

"Serious tech," Callie said. "We'd need explosives to get inside that vault. And I don't think we want to go there," she added with a glance toward Christina.

"No," Mal said dryly. "We don't." He thought for a moment. "Electric locks, I assume?"

"I think so. There was a keypad to enter. I'd be surprised if it was a safe with a dial."

Raine had been quiet during the exchange. Now he leaned forward. "If it's electronic, I can open it."

Mal frowned, because that was true. And it would be a damn good solution if it weren't for the fact that Raine had drawn the short end of the stick. One more time into the phoenix fire, and he wouldn't come out a sane man. He'd be hollow. Lost. Locked inside himself forever.

And that meant Mal couldn't risk him in the field. Not when the amulet would undoubtedly be protected by more than just the vault.

They needed him though, and although it might be dangerous, Mal knew there was one way to give Raine back some of the lives that had gone into the burn. To make the phoenix fire safe for him once again.

"Mal?" Raine pressed. "You know you need me."

Beside him, Callie squeezed her fingers so tight into Raine's wrist it left impressions. Her lips were pressed together in a thin line, but Mal had to give her credit for not protesting. She knew the risks—and she also knew the reward. And she was going to let him decide.

He looked at Liam, who cocked his head, clearly unsure. Mal took that as acquiescence—if Mal had a strong opinion on the matter, his co-leader would defer to him.

"You can go," he finally said. "But only on one condition."

Raine leaned back and crossed his arms over his chest, the colors of his tats vibrant in the soft lighting. "Yeah? What's that?"

"Christina has to agree."

"WHAT DO YOU mean I have to agree?"

I've been asking that question for the last five minutes, and now that we're finally alone in Mal's brownstone, I really want an answer.

"Because of what I'm going to ask you to do."

He's not looking at me as he speaks. Instead he's gone to the small table where he keeps liquor and glasses. He pours himself a generous shot of scotch, then slams it back, as if he's hoping to get at least a small buzz before that damned immortal metabolism sets in and sobers him right back up.

I cross to him, frowning. I don't understand what's going on, but I know that he's uncomfortable, and that somehow both Raine and I are involved.

And that makes me uncomfortable, too.

"Come here," I say. I take his hand, then lead

him to the sofa. I curl up against him, deliberately putting my back to his chest so that he understands he can talk freely and not censor his words based on the expression he thinks he's reading on my face.

Just one more tip from my mother's therapist. Who knew they'd be so handy?

"How much do you know about Raine?" He hasn't tried to shift position or turn me. But his arm is over my shoulder, and his fingers are lightly stroking my skin. I like it, this feeling of being together even when it's something difficult that we're facing.

"I know that he's with Callie. And I know what I remember from our past, but that was a long time ago. Just that he was a warrior, but he was also on the tech crew. Dual assignments. And I know that he's been your closest friend for a very long time. Even closer than Liam."

I feel him stiffen as I lean against him. "How do you know that?"

I shrug. "Observation. Deduction. You were already close. But then you lost me and he lost Livia. So it makes sense you'd bond. And I watched the two of you that very first night I came to the bar. It was clear you were old friends, and good ones. Just something about the way you moved. A familiarity, I guess."

"You're observant."

"One of the tricks of the trade. Hard to play a role if you haven't studied a role."

He's silent for a minute, and I wonder where all this is leading. Then he says, "Tell me about your mother."

It's my turn to tense. And despite what the shrink said, I shift on the couch so that I am facing him. "What the hell?"

He is completely unperturbed by my reaction. "Do you understand what she experienced when she went into her gray zones?"

Part of me wants to stand up and walk away, because I do not want to talk about this. But another part of me knows that Mal wouldn't be asking if there wasn't a reason. "I don't really know," I admit. "But I've had those kinds of episodes, too. As a kid—I told you, right? And I think it's sort of similar. It's just—nothing."

"Could you bear it? If she were still alive, but

constantly in that state? Or Brayden. Or me? Could you stand knowing that we were there, but not there? That we were lost in some hollow, mad world that might be empty, but that might be filled with horrible, dark things?"

"No." The word is full of pain, and I draw in a breath. "Why are you asking me this?"

"Because that's what will happen to Raine if he goes into the phoenix fire again."

I stare for a moment, not understanding. But then he explains. How too many times into the burn will hollow you out. How it's happened once already to a warrior named Samson. And how Raine knows that it will happen to him if he goes into the burn once more.

"That's why you didn't want him on the mission," I say. "He might get killed. And that's why it's up to me." I stand, then hug myself, remembering all too clearly the night when the weapon had risen dangerously high within me. I'd glowed with the power of it, and as I did, I'd touched Mal's back, and the ornate phoenix that represented almost ten lives lost and restored, vanished.

That was the night I'd realized that the underlying force that controlled the weapon was life, and that it has as much power to destroy as it does to heal.

"That was the night we were attacked," I say. "I was angry because I couldn't fight anymore. I was mad at the world and I was taking it out on you and me and everything around us, and I lost control. Do you remember how hot we were? How hard you fucked me? How much I wanted you?"

My throat feels tight and hot tears streak down my cheeks. I can't believe he's asking this of me. "Do you know how much of myself I exposed to you that night? How can you ask me to be that wild with someone else? For that matter, how can you justify the risk of me going ballistic just to save one man?"

He is on his feet and at my side in an instant. "No," he says. "God no." He turns me so that I have no choice but to face him. Even so, I can't quite manage to meet his eyes. "Listen to me, lover. I would never have you in another man's bed, and I will kill any man who touches you."

I shift my gaze, tentatively looking at his face.

"Then I don't understand what you want."

"I want us to make the weapon rise. I want to bring it out so you glow. And then I want you to touch Raine. To give him the weapon's energy. I think that's the key, and if I'm right, you can restore him."

"Oh." I run my fingers through my hair. That's definitely better than what I thought he'd suggested, but it was still pretty damn intimate, and I say as much to Mal.

"You're basically inviting him into our bedroom," I say. "Into our most intimate moments. I mean, if the weapon is rising then, well, so am I." My cheeks are burning and I feel ridiculously tongue-tied. At the same time, the realization that I am shying away from this disturbs me. Raine is a friend and key member of the brotherhood, and if I can restore him then what price is too high?

Mal pulls me close. "I understand. And you need to know that I wouldn't ask if it weren't important. Raine's one of our most powerful assets, yet the damn burn has practically castrated him."

I force a smile. "Possibly not the best choice of words under the circumstances."

I move away from him and start to pace, my mind in a whirl. "Look, here's the thing. And please, just let me say this, because I've been thinking a lot about teams. About you and me. And about me and the brotherhood.

"So if you're asking me as a member of the Phoenix Brotherhood, then I will do this for another teammate. Because the part of me that is Jaynie is still learning what's going on, but the Christina part remembers and trusts and respects you for your honor and your compassion and your sense of duty and loyalty."

I draw in a breath to fortify myself, then press on. "But if you're asking me to do this as your mate, your wife, then it's a little bit different. Because while I know that we went through a mating ceremony together, that was in another time and another dimension, and it has no meaning to me anymore."

I see the way my words hit him, the pain that crosses his face as quickly as the flick of a whip, and for a moment, I stumble. But I recover quickly and continue. "I don't feel the past, Mal. I *know* it, if that makes sense, but it's like something I learned from a book."

I know my words are harsh, but I need to be certain I have his attention. That he understands fully and completely everything I have to say.

"What I feel is you," I continue. "This intense connection between us? Good lord how I feel that. But the ritual? The mating? The binding that makes me yours? I'm sorry, but that just isn't real to me."

"What exactly are you telling me?" His expression is hard. His words are clipped. But I know that at the very least, he is listening. And that he is understanding me.

I draw a breath and walk closer to him. "I'm trying to tell you that I'm yours," I say softly. "Not because of a ceremony in some world I barely remember. Not because of a past that is more like a dream than a reality. But because of who you are now. What you are. And what we are together."

I watch his face as I speak, and I see the

wariness fading, replaced by a bloom of delight.

"I told you I loved you after you rescued me from the warehouse, and I meant it. But I didn't fully understand it. But I've had the chance to watch you more and to be with you, and I've seen the things in you that I love. Your tenderness, your loyalty. Your wit and charm. And the fact that you're amazing in bed doesn't hurt, either," I add, making him grin and, thankfully, lightening the moment.

"So if this is what you need to restore your team and to save your friend, then I will do it because you want it and need it. Even if it will be really, really weird."

His smile has been growing as I talk, and with my last he finally laughs.

"Thank you," he says simply, pulling me close and kissing me gently.

What I hear, of course, is *I love you.*

CHAPTER 8

I T IS WEIRD, but in the end it's not quite as weird as I anticipated.

For one thing, I have no time to worry about it. Because when I ask Mal when he wants to do this, his response is a flat, determined, "Now."

Second, when I go to talk to Callie, she does not share my reaction. There is no blush. There is no awkwardness. There is just relief, open and honest and painted all over her face.

And third, though I'd imagined some sort of harem-like setting with Raine tucked in a corner watching Mal and me, it is nothing like that.

Instead it is me, and it is Mal. And we are alone.

Even so, I can't stop thinking that we won't

remain alone. "It feels so strange," I say. "Letting him come in here. Letting him see us so intimately."

Mal tugs me to him, then peels off my shirt. I'm wearing a tank top underneath because, well, I insisted on staying at least somewhat clothed during this exercise. And, to be honest, I'm not entirely sure this is going to work. Because I'm not entirely sure that I can lose control. Not when I'm so self-conscious.

"You could just hurt me," I say. "Or he could."

He exhales, then steps back to look hard at me. "Does this bother you that much?"

I lick my lips. "Honestly? I'm not sure."

"He's not hurting you. And neither am I. If I had my way, no one would hurt you again."

"But doesn't it weird you out?" I ask, as his fingers work deftly on the button of my jeans. "Just a little?"

"No," he says, and the word is so firm that it sparks my curiosity.

"You've done this before. You've had a threesome with Raine." I've tried very hard not to think about all the women who must have shared Mal's bed when I was dead, or gone, or whatever you want to call it.

I lift a brow as I examine his face. For his part, he looks slightly perturbed. "I really don't think this is the time to discuss this. Lift your foot."

I do, and find myself in a tank top and my underwear.

"I don't know," I say, because now I have latched on to this new bit of information. And I like that, because it's taking my mind off my nerves. "I'm rather curious." I push him back onto the bed, and then straddle him. "Tell me about it, and I undress you. Don't tell me, and I'm just going to sit here."

He lifts a brow. "All right, yes. Raine and I have shared women."

"Did you like it?"

"It was expedient and it was a release," he says flatly.

"You liked it," I tease.

He rolls his eyes. "It was sex, nothing more. Sex. And control. And a way to forget, if only for a little bit, that we were in pain."

"I'm sorry," I say.

For a moment he looks a bit sad, but then he brushes my cheek. "But, okay, yes. I liked it. Frankly, that was the point."

I brush a kiss over his lips. "I'm glad. I don't like thinking of you so sad."

"It was hardly your fault."

"Mmm," I say. And since the mood is turning heavy, I ease back to the original topic. "So, next question. How many times?"

"Christina…"

"Hey, I think a woman has a right to know what her mate's up to when she's not around."

"Uh-huh." The corner of his mouth quirks up. "Jealous? Or curious?"

"A little of both," I admit.

"There's nothing to be jealous of," he says. "As for the number of times, I don't know. A dozen, maybe more. Three thousand years is a long time. And I killed you more times than I like to count."

My chest tightens. "Of course," I say. "You were with them after you killed me."

"That is when I was at my lowest, yes. That's

when I needed escape."

"Oh, Mal."

"Shhh. It's all better now. Everything is better now." He is stroking me through my clothes as he speaks, his fingers playing me as competently as a virtuoso at a keyboard. "And no, I will never share you. Which is why Raine will wait outside until he is invited in. And he stays only as long as necessary."

I don't know what I intended to say in response to that, but my words are soundly cut off by his mouth upon mine. The kiss is long and deep, and makes very clear that I am, as he has said, his. And when he breaks the kiss and meets my eyes, he says very slowly and firmly, "You understand?"

I nod.

"And you're not jealous?"

"No."

"And are you still, as you say, weirded out about being in my arms now? About me touching you like this while Raine waits just past our bedroom door?"

"No. Yes. A little," I gasp as he slips his finger under the band of my underwear to stroke my sex.

"A little, yes," he says. "And it excites you a little, too. Doesn't it? To know that there's someone out there. Someone who knows that I'm touching you. That I'm teasing you. That I'm going to take you right to the edge, and that even though I'm going to share a tiny part of you, that you are mine and only mine."

"I—yes." The admission is a whisper, but it is also a balm. It washes away the awkwardness leaving only desire and heat and a building fire.

Mal's touches become wilder and I arch up to meet him. And he is taking me so far, so far, so very far until—

"Mal! Oh, god, Mal!"

"Hold on, baby. Let it take you. I've got you. I won't let it get out of control."

I believe him—I do—and yet I don't know how he can make such a promise against something so wild and wicked. Something hard and hot and powerful.

Something that wants to destroy us both.

But he keeps touching me, keeps playing me. And desire curls through me. Passion rises within me. And, oh Christ, I'm right there, an orgasm building and the weapon looming right behind it, and though I trust Mal, I don't know how the hell he is ever going to manage to back this down. Because it's too much.

It's too damn much.

And then I am glowing, the power seeping out of me, and it's too strong, it's too—

And then Raine is there.

I don't know how Mal called him in, but he's right there in front of me, facing me. And I clutch his arms and hold tight even as Mal presses up from behind me, his chest against my back, his hands cupping my breasts. And, yes, I feel the power flow.

I cry out, consumed by pain, by passion, by the wildness of this moment, then I lean forward, breathing hard, pressing my forehead against Raine's. I'm burning. The glow rushing through me and into him, as if being drawn into a vacuum. Maybe that's what the tats are, not just a marker, but a hollow. A vacuum that the life inside me is rushing to fill.

And it's so wild.

So powerful.

And it's growing and building until I no

longer feel part of the world, and am simply spinning, spinning, spin—

"*Christina!*"

Then he's there. *Mal.* Drawing back my energy as well as the weapon's. Holding me tight. Urging it all back down again. Holding me close. And never, ever letting go.

I breathe deep, in and out, until I am sure that I am steady again. Then I turn in Mal's arms to see Raine in front of us on the bed. And his arms that used to be fully sleeved are now nothing but clear, tanned skin.

Callie stands across the room, her back to the wall, her hand over her mouth. And even at this distance I can see the tears that stream down her cheek.

It's over.

It worked.

And, yes, it was worth it.

Slowly, Raine leans forward, then kisses my cheek. "Thank you."

"You're welcome," I say, then grin at all three of them. My mate. My friends. "Now let's go kick a little fuerie butt."

CHAPTER 9

U NFORTUNATELY, THERE IS very little butt-kicking to be had.

We go to the store and, as advertised, Raine is able to break in.

And though we've come prepared for a full-out battle with the fuerie's human minions, we don't suffer even a broken fingernail. Instead, we're able to waltz right into the vault, take the gemstone, and get the hell out of there with absolutely nothing happening.

Honestly, it is all very anticlimactic.

The reason, of course, becomes clear once we return to Number 36.

"It's an opal," Callie says. "But it's not the amulet. Not the one my dad had at his store for

Raine."

"I don't get it," I say. "I saw it. Shining bright on the map in my head. If it's not the amulet, what is it? Why did I see it?"

"Another supercharged gemstone?" Bray suggests. He'd not been part of the raid, of course, but he'd insisted on staying until Dagny returned safe and sound. Mal and Liam agreed with very little debate, and I'm glad. I'm still straddling my two lives—Christina, Jaynie—and it's nice to have pieces of both with me.

"What do you mean?" Jessica asks.

"Well, the amulet has all this power, right? And we know that regular gems can have energy, too. But Jay doesn't see every diamond in the world on her mind map. She saw just this one specific stone. So I'm guessing it's a plant."

"A plant?" I say.

"A trick. A bluff." He looks between me and Jessica, and then exhales, obviously surprised that we aren't following him. "I think these fuerie dudes must have jerry rigged this opal. Gave it more energy or something so that they could fool Jaynie."

"But they weren't even laying in wait," Asher said. "So what's the point?"

My stomach twists unpleasantly with a sudden understanding. "I think I know. Hang on."

I close my eyes, focus, and pull up the map. It's easy this time, my skills more honed. And, as I suspected, there are dozens and dozens of colored lights.

My shoulders sag as I open my eyes. "They're hiding the amulet. This one was a test to see if it worked, if I sensed it. And we took the bait. Now there are dozens of so-called amulets floating on the map, all over the globe. And I have no way of knowing which one is the real one."

"Fuck." Mal's curse is soft, but heartfelt.

"I second that," Liam says. "But this isn't entirely bad. If they can manipulate the energy of the stones, then so can we. And if we can do that, then we can trap the fuerie when we hunt them. No more letting them poison the fabric of this world by dissipating into the ether. And no more bouncing to another body when one is close enough to host them. We kill them. We catch them. We keep them bound."

"The tech team tried that before," Raine says. "A couple of thousand years ago. We couldn't manage it. The energy pattern in this world won't do it, and now that we're bound in humans, our energy won't accomplish it either."

"But the fuerie's energy can be used to manipulate a gemstone," Liam said. "We've just witnessed it."

"But if we don't have the fuerie's energy..." I trail off, confused. It sounds like a chicken and the egg problem. We need a fuerie to turn earthen gems into traps. But we can't get a fuerie because we have no gemstone.

"Maybe not," Liam says. "But I think we have something better." He's looking hard at me.

"The weapon," I say.

He nods. "How better to turn a weapon to good than to use it to trap the enemy?"

I look at Mal, and he nods slowly.

"All right," I say. "If Mal's there to make sure I stay safe, I can do that. But all this does is help with the work the brotherhood is already doing—hunting the fuerie. We still need the real amulet if we're going to get the weapon out of me."

"True," Mal agrees. "We need to figure out how you can identify it. How you can see it apart from all the others scattered across your map."

"Every gemstone has a unique energy pattern," Ash says.

"So if Christina can figure out how to isolate each pattern…" Dagny continues.

I frown. "Except that isolating them doesn't do me any good unless I know what I'm looking for. It's like looking at a box of crayons and now knowing if I'm supposed to choose the red or the green one. Unless I know, seeing the crayons doesn't much matter."

"And without the amulet," Callie says, "you can't figure out the pattern."

"So we're back to square one," Jessica says.

I lean against Mal and exhale. "Well, shit."

MAL HAD NEVER been one to shy away from a fight, but he couldn't ever remember being so grateful that a mission had turned out to be so completely danger-free.

And, dear god, he couldn't keep his hands off Christina. Couldn't stop touching her. Couldn't stop reassuring himself that even as time continued to pass, she was still there beside him. Still breathing. Still his.

"I'm yours."

Those simple words had cut through him with a power that no fuerie's whip ever had. And the pure force of his reaction had surprised him. Of course she was his—she had been for millennia. But to hear her say it. To hear her mean it. To truly understand the depth of her emotion for him notwithstanding the mating ritual or the brotherhood or any of it had truly humbled him.

Christ, he loved her.

And it wasn't until they'd returned from the mission to find the false amulet that he realized how truly terrifying love could be. Because he'd worried every damn step of the way, and only relaxed when they'd returned safe to Number 36.

"You're quiet tonight," she said. They were

still in the VIP lounge, but they'd moved to a back booth after the meeting had broken. She'd tried to slide off his lap to the cushion beside him, but he'd held her close, locking her within his embrace.

"Just thinking."

"Yeah? About what?"

"About how much I love you."

Her grin had been mischievous, but now her expression shifted, turning both warm and serious. "I love you, too," she said. "But?"

He laughed. "No buts. I love you fully and completely. *But*," he added, as he stroked her cheek, "you're not immortal. I can't risk losing you. We got lucky in Orlov's store. But if there had been fuerie or even their minions..."

She stiffened in his arms. "We've talked about this before. I'll do what's best for the team and the brotherhood, Mal. I learned my lesson about being selfish. But you can't be selfish, either." She leaned in and kissed him, and his heart twisted because he knew what she was going to say, and he knew that she was right. "You can't keep me out of the mix simply because you're afraid. That doesn't help the team, either."

"I know," he said. "But dear god, it would kill me to lose you again."

Her smile was both knowing and sad. "I am immortal, though. If I die I will come back to you."

A wall of emotion seemed to rise up around him, and he had to fight his way through it just to answer her. "Don't even think like that. It could be a thousand years before you return, and when you do, you may not know me at all. I can't even bear the thought of it."

She shook her head. "No," she said softly. "Neither can I. But unless we get the weapon out of me, it will happen. Either by violence or by nature." She licked her lips. "I'm going to grow old, Mal. Every day, I am growing old. And in what feels like the blink of an eye to you, I will leave this earth. We don't even know what will happen after that. Does natural death change anything? Will the weapon still be in me? Will I come back?"

She blinked and a tear trickled down her

cheek, and he felt like a complete ass for starting this whole conversation. For getting soppy and sentimental. For not just focusing on the problem at hand and doing whatever it took to move forward with getting the weapon out of her.

"It's going to be okay," he said firmly. "*We're* going to be okay. Trust, remember? You have to trust me."

He kissed her hard, but still felt like an ass. He was being weak when he should be strong, but goddammit, she was the only thing in the entire world that made him feel vulnerable. The only thing that could shatter him. And though he didn't know how it was possible, with every day that passed, he needed her more.

CHAPTER 10

S OMETHING WAKES ME from a sound sleep
the next morning, and it takes me a few
moments to realize that it is my own thoughts.

Callie.

I roll over to tell Mal, but he isn't in the bed,
and so I search the floor for the T-shirt and yoga
pants I dropped there last night, then pad out of
the bedroom to find him.

He's in the kitchen reading the newspaper as
he waits for the coffee to brew. He's wearing
nothing but boxers and looks so incredibly sexy
that he could easily be mistaken for a model
advertising the espresso machine. And when he
looks up at me and captures me in the heat of
that slow, sensual smile, I'm surprised that I do

not melt into a pile of goo right then and there.

"Well, good morning," he says. "Guess who's not getting breakfast in bed after all."

"I'm going to go out on a limb and say me." I take a seat on one of the barstools, then gratefully take the coffee he offers me. "Ask me why I'm awake."

"All right," he says agreeably. "Why are you awake?"

"Callie."

His brow furrows. "Is she here? I didn't hear the door."

"No, I was thinking about her. About her dad, really. And about the amulet."

"Go on." I see the subtle change as he shifts seamlessly from morning banter to work mode. Now, he doesn't look like a model in boxers, he looks like an executive in a suit—despite the boxers. And I can't help but be impressed.

"It's just that her dad found it once."

Mal's mouth curves down thoughtfully. "Go on."

"All these different stones I'm seeing, they each have their own energy. And I don't know how to tell them apart when I look at them in my mind. But what if Oliver does? He's held the amulet. He's touched it. Maybe he'd recognize the pattern?"

I take another sip of my coffee as I study his face, trying to guess how he will respond to my suggestion.

"If that's the case, then shouldn't Callie recognize it, too?"

I shake my head. "We've talked a lot since I came here, and she's told me all about her dad and how she ended up here with the brotherhood. She's never actually held the amulet. Just the box. I don't think it would be the same."

He's silent for a moment as he turns away. I watch as he puts the coffee beans up, then takes a bagel out of the bread box and slices it. As soon as he's pushed the lever down on the toaster, he turns his attention back to me. "It's a good idea, lover, but Oliver had a stroke. He's in a nursing home, and he doesn't talk."

"He does to Callie. He's got Livia inside him, too, just like she does, and they're connected. And we both know that we're capable of moving energy back and forth." I think of what happened with Raine—of how Mal gave me his energy for control and I gave Raine the weapon's energy to heal.

"You're thinking that she should talk to your dad, and you should eavesdrop on the conversation?"

I lift a shoulder. "More or less."

"All right, then," he says as the bagel pops up, as if in punctuation of our conversation. "It's a good idea, and frankly I don't have a better one."

A SERIES OF strokes left Oliver Sinclair incapacitated, and now he spends his life in a bed, not speaking, not interacting with the staff, but simply being. Despite all that, his room at the nursing home is surprisingly cheerful. It's full of fresh flowers, and unlike the rest of the building which has the antiseptic smell of a hospital, his room smells fresh and clean, the scent of the flowers mixing with the smell of fresh paint.

"Raine and I spent a weekend trying to make it nice," Callie said. "I think the ladies on staff think it's silly since he hasn't opened his eyes, but he's seen it through mine. Not that I can explain that to them. Besides," she adds with a casual lift of her shoulder, "even if we couldn't communicate the way we can, he can still smell the flowers. And what does it hurt to make his room look nice?"

"I think it's great," I say gently. I was never close to my mom, but she *was* my mom, and losing her so horrifically to suicide had messed me up. I can't imagine how it must feel to lose a parent and yet not really lose them. And in that moment, I realize that it was that exact fate that she had feared for Raine. That he would be physically there, but mentally not.

With Oliver, the fact that they shared part of Livia's essence allowed them to communicate despite his strokes. With Raine, the hollow would have left both Raine and Callie with nothing.

I've mostly gotten over the weirdness of giving back Raine his lives, but that small revelation pushes the rest of the awkwardness

ed now. And though I cannot feel the amulet, I can feel him. And if he can see the map in my mind, then maybe—just maybe—this will work after all.

I draw in a breath, trying to focus.

It's hard at first, but then the map appears. It fills my head. Fills the room.

And then, yes, it fills with light.

"The orange flickers are—"

"The fuerie," he says. "Yes, I see. And the colors are gemstones." He chuckles. "Clever bastards aren't they?"

"They tested it first," I say. "Enhanced the energy in a gemstone so that I would think it was the amulet. They didn't even lie in wait for us. It was a just a test. Just a test to see if they could hide the real thing."

"How did they keep the real one from flashing onto the map?"

"Me," I admit. "Inexperience."

I remember how I'd seen another hint of color, but it was overwhelmed by the orange glow surrounding it. "They'd gathered around the amulet, their energy pouring over the amulet's. If I knew then what I know now, I would have realized it."

"And now you cannot look for the gemstone that is surrounded by the fuerie, because they will know now that you figured out that trick."

"But at least that means the amulet is not as well guarded," Callie says. "They may have humans watching it, but there can't be too many fuerie around it or else Christina would see."

"And what do we see now?" Oliver asks, and I realize that during this conversation, the orange glows on the map have faded.

"How—"

"It is your map," Oliver says. "You can learn to control it."

"So these are all gemstones?" Callie asks. The map is littered with colored lights.

"They are. Now reach out," Oliver says. "Reach out and feel each one."

I do—and it is as if I am floating over the map, over the colors. I feel the unique energy of each stone. Some cold and harsh. Others warm and flowing.

And then, yes, a slight tingle. A tickle almost.

Just like the kiss of a butterfly.

"You've done well," Oliver says.

"Thank you." I am swimming with relief. It's across the country in California. Not close, but we can get there.

And with any luck, the fuerie won't see us coming.

"Tired now," he says.

"Rest," I say. "And thank you."

CHAPTER 11

N OW THAT I know the amulet's signature, I'm able to hone in on it without Oliver's help. I do that five times over the next few hours, getting closer and closer each time.

It's in a large house in the California dessert, about twenty miles out from Palm Springs. Isolated. Easily monitored by electronic surveillance and probably rigged with all sorts of traps. And though I cannot see them, I'm betting that it's full of human guards who are willing to give their lives to protect the stone.

As for the fuerie, I see none within a ten-mile radius. If that holds, we can get in, get the amulet, and get out before they arrive.

But that doesn't make the mission less dangerous—their human minions are dangerous, too. And if they manage to take out the brotherhood's team before we've acquired the stone, then it's all over. The team will come back, of course, but it will be too late. And considering the fuerie's end game, I'm certain the humans will be under orders to torture me. To do whatever it takes to trigger the weapon.

"All right," Liam says after I reassure them all once again that the amulet hasn't moved. "You have your assignments. Wheels up in thirty minutes."

We're in Mal's living room, and all around us the other members of the brotherhood pack up their notes and head off to the various tasks of gathering equipment, readying the aircraft, and contacting brotherhood members in California who will be joining the raid.

Throughout all the hustle and bustle, Mal says nothing. He just sits in the leather armchair that dominates one side of the room. There is a floor lamp behind him, and the light it emits casts him in shadows, as if tinting his gorgeous features with sadness.

I wait until everyone has left, and then go kneel on the floor in front of him. "You don't want me to go."

"No," he says. "I really don't."

"We both know I have to," I say softly. "They might move the amulet. You'll need me to find it. And if we take the other six amulets with us—"

"No. It's too risky. If it's a trap and they get those other six from us, then it really is the end."

I nod, because he's right; we need all seven to draw the weapon out of me.

"We get the seventh. We bring it back. And then we take care of you." He strokes my cheek. "And you don't take any unnecessary chances."

"I won't," I promise. I'm on my knees, my hands pressed against his thighs for leverage. Now, he pulls me up to face him.

"Christina." That's all he says. Just my name. But it is like a soliloquy of pain and fear, and I am not expecting it when he pulls me close. When he kisses me so wild and violently that every cell in my body fires with desire. I cling to him, wanting to deepen the kiss. Wanting more—so much more.

But even as desire stirs within me—even as I feel the weapon shimmer and come to life—I know that there is not time. Right now, we have to go.

Right now, we have to fight.

And I can only hope that the next time he touches me like this the weapon will be gone and I can finally, *finally*, lose myself fully and completely in my husband's arms.

And that, I think, is something worth fighting for.

CHAPTER 12

W E DESCEND ON the house in darkness, moving slowly, fully armed.

I feel as though I've joined a paramilitary organization, and have been thrust into my first mission with no training. Which, frankly, is more or less the reality.

But Mal is at my side, and so I am not nervous. Not too much, anyway.

We make it through the gates with Raine's help, and we go in slowly, carefully. Our team consists of the New York group, minus Callie who stayed in New York to oversee the operation, and a team from the Los Angeles office of the brotherhood.

On the whole, we are a group of eighteen,

and I am amazed that we are moving almost completely unseen.

Though the place was unguarded when we left New York, now I see over thirty fuerie when I scan the map. And it's anybody's guess how many humans they have working as backup.

I'm not surprised. After all, this is it. This is the amulet. With all seven, we can pull the weapon out of me and bind it. With it, we can bind the fuerie. With it, we can manipulate the universe and return to our dimension.

Once we have the seventh amulet, we have essentially won. Everything that comes after is just clean-up.

So, yeah, if I were the fuerie, I'd be protecting it, too.

Surprisingly, though, they don't attack.

The reason becomes clear soon enough—the place is booby-trapped.

The ground is a minefield, and as I watch, horrified, two of the California team members get blow to bits.

"Oh, god. Will they—"

"They will," Mal assures me, even as the

phoenix fire starts to flare around their scattered remains. "But you won't. Raine!"

"On it," he says, then kneels down and presses his hand to the ground.

"What's he doing?"

"Talking to the mines. Shutting them down."

"Seriously?"

"Seriously," Mal says once Raine rises. He takes my hand. "It's safe now, but the explosion will have alerted whoever is in the house. Hurry, and stay low."

We get inside, along with a dozen more of the team. The rest remain outside, surrounding the location to guard against anyone coming late to the party.

Immediately, we are attacked as five fuerie with their whips extended launch themselves at us. Mal shoves me out of the way just in time to prevent me from taking the brunt of a lashing.

He holds them off with his fire sword until Liam arrives beside him. "Go! Let Christina lead you to the amulet. We'll hold them off."

Mal takes my hand and I point toward the stairs. I didn't see the interior of the house on the map, but somehow I know that is where we need to be.

Raine follows, assigned to stay with us in case we need him to enter a vault.

As it happens, we do.

But it is rigged, too, and as soon as the door opens, an arrow springs out, catching him in the throat. I scream as he falls, but Mal only pushes me behind him. "The amulet," he says. "We need to get the amulet."

My pulse is pounding with terror, and all I want to do is tug Mal away from here. But I realize that the only reason we're here—the only reason Raine suffered such a horrific injury—is to get this stone. We have to get it. For me. For the brotherhood. For the world.

"Got it!" Triumphantly, Mal holds up his hand, the stone hidden in his fist and the golden chain dangling.

I turn to look at Raine even as the first sparks of the phoenix fire begin to dance around him. "Should we—?"

"He'll be fine," he says. His voice is low. Rough. And more serious than I have ever heard it. "We have to go. I have to get you out of here."

We do, racing with the amulet toward the exit as Mal calls into his headphone for the team to cover us as we retreat, and for another team to enter and cover Raine while the phoenix fire regenerates him.

I start to ask why, since Mal has already said that Raine will be fine. But then I realize—he will come back to life, yes. But that doesn't mean the fuerie can't capture him. Can't torture him.

And immortality can last a long, long time in a torture chamber.

The realization haunts me, and I stumble. I reach for Mal, but even as I do another spear zings out from the end of the hallway. Its trajectory is straight and true—and I know with absolute surety that it is going to impale me.

There is a blur of motion and almost instantaneously I am shoved sideways. I slam hard onto the ground, and by the time I have shifted to look up again, I see Mal get thrown backwards, thrust hard against the wall by the force of the spear that he has taken dead-on in the heart.

I scream, the sound ripping my throat and piercing the air even as he stumbles, then falls to the ground.

I crawl to him, clawing my way across the ground to his side. He looks at me, the light fading from his gray eyes, and when he opens his mouth to whisper my name, I see the small bubble of blood on his lips.

His eyes go flat—and he is still.

Mal!!!

This time, I'm not even sure that I have screamed aloud. All I know is that his name fills me. And even as I cry for him, the phoenix fire starts to grow around him.

He's coming back. I know that.

He. Is. Coming. Back.

I can focus. I can do this. Because right now, my mission is to get the amulet out of here.

I just have to move. I just have to *go*.

I try to rise, but I'm still in shock. And when I finally do manage to stumble to my feet, it is too late.

I'm tackled by a huge man with muscles of steel and a face of writhing flame. I start to cry out for help, but he slaps me across the face, silencing my cry and knocking me to the ground.

I scream, then roll to my side, prepared to defend myself. But he is not there. Instead, he has reached into the circle of flame and retrieved the amulet from beside Mal's burning body.

And then, dammit, he starts running back down the hallway.

No.

No. Fucking. Way.

I scramble to my feet, but he has too much of a lead on me. I know that I won't catch him. And yet I can't let him get away. I don't know what to do, and in that moment I feel more alone than I ever have, trapped in that house, surrounded by the fuerie, by the brotherhood.

And with Mal not there to help me.

Except he is there.

He is right beside me. Engulfed in the phoenix fire, yes, but it is still him. And though I have no idea what inspires me, I reach through the phoenix flame and touch Mal's burning body. I remember the time with Callie and her father. I'd felt what he felt. And he'd seen what I'd seen.

Can I do it? Can I borrow Mal's strength? His power?

Can I manage to get the amulet and not destroy the world?

I concentrate, closing my eyes, imagining that he is there. Imagining that he is touching me. Giving me energy. Giving me strength. Giving me *him*.

I let it all gather inside me, building and building even as the weapon grows and grows, too.

I'm terrified that I'll lose control, but I have Mal's strength to guide me. To hold me.

And I have to trust that our strength together will be enough.

I let it grow, I let it build. I let the weapon— dark and dangerous—rise up inside me.

I tell myself this will work. That I can do this. That I will not—will not—will not destroy the world.

Because if I do, then I will be destroying Mal, as well. And I cannot even bear the thought.

The power is wild inside me. Filling me. Claiming me.

I can wait no longer—and with a massive burst of willpower, I use the growing power of the weapon as a catapult to push Mal's power out of me.

To make a forcefield.

To slam the air back so that the fuerie who is racing down the hall with the amulet is ripped off his feet and thrown against the wall, unable to resist the force of the invisible wall that I've sent rushing his way.

He falls, limp, to the ground.

I allow myself less than a second for self-congratulations and then I race that direction. I grab the amulet, my mind reeling from exhaustion.

And then, as I see Liam sprinting up the stairs, his expression hard, my knees go weak and the world goes dark.

CHAPTER 13

I WAKE BACK in New York, feeling light and happy and, strangely, more like myself than I ever have.

Mal is beside me, and I see the worry fade from his stormy gray eyes as I smile up at him.

"How do you feel?"

"Alive," I say. "Really, really alive."

"It's gone," he says. "We pulled the weapon out. We bound it. And we've locked the amulets away, seven pieces protected in seven locations. Do you remember?"

I close my eyes. All I remember is the sensation of being held. Of being loved.

"I remember you were with me. Other than that, I don't remember it at all." I sit up, suddenly realizing. "So does that mean that I'm—I mean, will I—"

His smile blooms, and I know that he understands my question. Not only that, but I know the answer simply from the joy on his face.

"Yes," he says, then tugs down the neck of the sleep shirt that I am wearing. I crane my neck and bend my shoulder and when I do I can barely—just barely—see the small tattoo of a phoenix on my shoulder blade. The tattoo that now marks me as one of the brotherhood. As immortal.

I sigh with relief, and brush away the tears that spill down my cheeks.

"There's a debrief in two hours," Mal says. "You should rest until then."

I laugh, then slide closer to him. "Trust me," I say. "I have no intention of resting."

"Christina..." I hear the protest in his voice, and I know that he is concerned. But there is heat there, too—and that means that I can convince him.

"Hush," I say as I press my finger to his lips. "There's only one thing I need from you right now, and that is for you to make love to me. Wholly and completely," I add as reach for my sleep shirt and pull it off. I'm naked now, and I move onto his lap, my fingers going to the buttons on his shirt. "I want everything, Mal, and I want you to take me there. Take me to the edge," I whisper as I push his shirt open and press my palm to his chest. "Take me to the edge, Mal, and then push me over."

He requires no more convincing, and without another word he rolls me over so that I am flat on the bed and he is straddling me. "Do you have any idea how much I want this?" he asks, and I can only laugh.

"I'm guessing about as much as I do."

"This won't be slow," he says. "It won't be gentle."

"No." My pulse has kicked up, my body is on fire. Right then, I think I could come simply from the sound of his voice and the anticipation of his touch. The thought scares me at first, and then I remember—I don't have to be scared anymore. I don't have to hold back any longer.

"Please," I beg. "Don't wait. I don't think I

can't stand one more second of waiting."

He doesn't disappoint, and I arch up to meet him as he thrusts easily inside me. I am ready for him, hot and wet and open, and I gasp with delight at the feel of him, so deep and so hard, and so deliciously, sweetly, wonderfully unrestrained.

"Don't hold back," I say. "Please, don't hold back at all." I need to feel it all. Fast and wild and hard. I need to experience what I already know—that I can explode in Mal's arms without the world shattering around us.

That I can lose myself in passion and not lose myself entirely.

As always, he understands what I need, and he thrusts relentlessly into me, and as our bodies piston together, I meet each thrust, each motion driving me higher and higher and higher until I feel him tighten inside me. His release triggers mine, and I explode in a cacophony of light and color. And then slowly, so deliciously slow, I drift back down into myself and into reality.

And, yes, into Mal's arms.

"Mmm," I say, snuggling close and making

small noises of pure satisfaction.

He brushes a kiss over my temple, and I gather my strength to roll on top of him. I want to see his face. His eyes.

"Thank you," I say.

"For what?"

"For saving me. For loving me."

His smile is just a little smug. "How can I not? You're mine."

"Will you do something for me?"

"Anything," he says.

"Will you make love to me again?"

This time, he laughs. "Lover, it will be my pleasure."

MAL STOOD WITH Liam by the bar in the Dark Pleasures VIP lounge and looked his friends gathered in front of him. His team. His brothers.

"We have all seven amulets," he said, "but now there are decisions that need to be made. We can take it out into the world when we hunt the fuerie and use it to bind them, but that imposes a significant risk."

"The weapon?" Callie asked. "The weapon is bound by the amulets. If we take the amulets out when we hunt, there's a risk that the fuerie could attack and reacquire the weapon?"

"Exactly," Liam said. "Mal and I think it's better to keep the amulets split up. Right now, they're in seven vaults, protected by seven of the brotherhood's cells. That reduces the risk of the fuerie reacquiring all seven of the amulets and releasing the weapon."

"That's fine for the weapon," Asher said. "But now we can't use the amulets to bind the fuerie."

"True," Mal said. "But before the California mission, Christina altered the energy spectrum on over one hundred gemstones. We can use those stones when we hunt. And we can bind the fuerie inside them."

"Fair enough," Ash said. "But now we're back to hunting the way we used to."

"Without the map in Christina," Raine elaborated, "we have no easy way of finding the fuerie." He glanced at her. "Not that I'm saying we should put the weapon back. But that was a nifty trick for our wheelhouse, and now it's gone."

She only frowned, and so Mal hurried on, afraid that she would volunteer to absorb the weapon again. And that was something he would never agree to. It might be harder on the brotherhood without the map in her head, but nothing would compare to how hard it would be on him if he lost her again.

"We can rely on Dante and the others like him," Mal said. "It's not ideal, but it worked for us for thousands of years. And as we all know so well, we have plenty of time on our hands."

"No," Christina said softly, and Mal clenched his fists at his sides. "That's not—"

"We're not having this argument now," Mal said, his voice low but firm.

"But Mal—"

"*No.* We are not putting the weapon inside you. You're at risk when the weapon is in you, and even the opportunity to see the fuerie across the globe isn't worth the downside. Dammit," he added, though he'd had no intention to reveal so much of himself to the rest of his team, "do you think I would risk you like that? You don't get reborn in the phoenix fire when the weapon is inside you. Do you think I could live without you again should the worst happen?"

"You don't have to." It was the softness of her voice that finally captured his attention. "That's what I've been trying to tell you, Mal. You don't have to risk me at all."

"What are you saying?" The question came from Raine, but it was to Mal that Christina spoke.

"I can still see them."

"What?" Mal's voice merged with Liam's.

"I told you—the weapon's source is life. And life changes people. And I guess with all the time it was trapped in me it finally changed me, too."

"You can see them?" Jessica asked, and Christina nodded.

"I close my eyes and I can see the map. And they're out there, just like a stain on the world."

"So we can find them," Mal said slowly. "And with the gems that we've made, we can bind them, too."

He looked out at the team, at each of them in

turn, his gaze finally settling on Christina.

"Do you all know what this means?"

Her smile was slow and very smug. "Yes," she said. "Game on."

I hope you enjoyed the third part of Mal and Christina's story, which follows Part 1, Find Me in Darkness and Part 2, Find Me in Pleasure. I'd be thrilled if you'd leave a review at your favorite retailer!

And be sure to find out what happens next in the series. Dante's story, Caress of Pleasure is coming soon! Learn more at my website!

And if you missed Callie and Raine's story, Caress of Darkness, be sure to grab a copy now! You can learn more at my website.

Finally, don't close this book yet! Keep reading for the first chapter of Caress of Darkness, along with the first chapter of Tainted, my sexy urban fantasy romance, and Carpe Demon: Adventures of a Demon-Hunting Soccer Mom, the first book in the bestselling series that is now in development as a TV series for the CW network!

CARESS OF DARKNESS
EXCERPT

Please enjoy this first chapter from Raine and Callie's story:

Caress of Darkness

A Dark Pleasures novella

By

Julie Kenner

CHAPTER 1

"WHO THE FUCK are you?"

I jump, startled by the voice—deep and male and undeniably irritated—that echoes across the forest of boxes scattered throughout my father's SoHo antique store.

"Who am I?" I repeat as I stand and search the shadows for the intruder. "Who the hell are you?"

There is more bravado in my voice than I feel, especially when I finally see the man who has spoken. He is standing in the shadows near the front door—a door that I am damn sure I locked after putting the Closed sign in the window and settling in for a long night of inventory and packing.

He is tall, well over six feet, with a lean, muscular build that is accentuated by the faded jeans that hug his thighs and the simple white T-shirt that reveals muscled arms sleeved with tattoos.

His casual clothes, inked skin, and close-shaved head hint at danger and rebellion, but those traits are contrasted by a commanding, almost elegant, presence that seems to both fill the room and take charge of it. This is a man who would be equally at ease in a tux as a T-shirt. A man who expects the world to bend to his will, and if it doesn't comply, he will go out and bend it himself.

I see that confidence most potently in his face, all sharp lines and angles that blend together into a masterpiece now dusted with the shadow of a late afternoon beard. He has the kind of eyes that miss nothing, and right now they are hard and assessing. They are softened, however, by the kind of long, dark lashes that most women would kill for.

His mouth is little more than a hard slash across his features, but I see a hint of softness, and when I find myself wondering how those lips would feel against my skin, I realize that I have been staring and yank myself firmly from my reverie.

"I asked you a question," I snap, more harshly than I intended. "Who are you, and how did you get in here?"

"Raine," he says, striding toward me. "Rainer Engel. And I walked in through the front door."

"I locked it." I wipe my now-sweaty hands on my dusty yoga pants.

"The fact that I'm inside suggests otherwise."

He has crossed the store in long, efficient strides, and now stands in front of me. I catch his scent, all musk and male, sin and sensuality, and feel an unwelcome ache between my thighs.

Not unwelcome because I don't like sex. On the contrary, I'd have to label myself a fan, and an overenthusiastic one at that. Because the truth is that I've spent too many nights in the arms of too many strangers trying to fill some void in myself.

I say "some void" because I don't really know what I'm searching for. A connection, I guess, but at the same time I'm scared of finding one and ending up hurt, which is why I shy from traditional "my friend has a friend" kind of dating, and spend more time than I should in bars and clubs. And that means that while I might be enjoying a series of really good lays, I'm not doing anything more than using sex as a Band-Aid.

At least, that is what my therapist, Kelly, back home in Austin says. And since I'm a lawyer and not a shrink, I'm going to have to take her word on that.

"We're closed," I say firmly. Or, rather, I intend to say firmly. In fact, my voice comes out thin, suggesting a question rather than a command.

Not that my tone matters. The man— *Raine*—seems entirely uninterested in what I have to say.

He cocks his head slightly to one side, as if taking my measure, and if the small curve of that sensual mouth is any indication, he likes what he sees. I prop a hand on my hip and stare back defiantly. I know what I look like—and I know that with a few exceptions, men tend to go stupid when I dial it up.

The ratty law school T-shirt I'm wearing is tight, accenting breasts that I'd cursed in high school, but that had become a boon once I started college and realized that my ample tits, slender waist, and long legs added up to a combination that made guys drool. Add in wavy blonde hair and green eyes and I've got the kind of cheerleader-esque good looks that make so many of the good old boy lawyers in Texas think that I've got cotton candy for brains.

And believe me when I say that I'm not shy about turning their misogynistic stereotype to my advantage, both in the courtroom and out of it.

"You're Callie." His voice conveys absolute certainty, as if his inspection confirmed one of the basic facts of the universe. Which, since I *am* Callie, I guess it did. But how the hell he knows who I am is beyond me.

"Your father talks about you a lot," Raine says, apparently picking up on my confusion. His eyes rake over me as he speaks, and my skin prickles with awareness, as potent as if his fingertip had stroked me. "A lawyer who lives in

Texas with the kind of looks that make a father nervous, balanced by sharp, intelligent eyes that reassure him that she's not going to do anything stupid."

"You know my father."

"I know your father," he confirms.

"And he told you that about me?"

"The lawyer part. The rest I figured out all on my own." One corner of his mouth curves up. "I have eyes, after all." Those eyes are currently aimed at my chest, and I say a silent thank you to whoever decided that padded bras were a good thing because otherwise he would certainly see how hard and tight my nipples have become.

"University of Texas School of Law. Good school." He lifts his gaze from my chest to my face, and the heat I see in those ice blue eyes seems to seep under my skin, melting me a bit from the inside out. "Very good."

I lick my lips, realizing that my mouth has gone uncomfortably dry. I've been working as an assistant district attorney for the last two years. I've gotten used to being the one in charge of a room. And right now, I'm feeling decidedly off-kilter, part of me wanting to pull him close, and the other wanting to run as far and as fast from him as I can.

Since neither option is reasonable at the moment, I simply take a step back, then find myself trapped by the glass jewelry case, now pressing against my ass.

I clear my throat. "Listen, Mr. Engel, if you're looking for my father—"

"I am, and I apologize for snapping at you when I came in, but I was surprised to see that the shop was closed, and when I saw someone other than Oliver moving inside, I got worried."

"I closed early so that I could work without being interrupted."

A hint of a smile plays at his mouth. "In that case, I'll also apologize for interrupting. But Oliver asked me to come by when I got back in town. I'm anxious to discuss the amulet that he's located."

"Oh." I don't know why I'm surprised. He obviously hadn't come into the store looking for me. And yet for some reason the fact that I've suddenly become irrelevant rubs me the wrong way.

Clearly, I need to get a grip, and I paste on my best customer service smile. "I'm really sorry, but my dad's not here."

"No? I told him I'd come straight over." I can hear the irritation in his voice. "He knows how much I want this piece—how much I'm willing to pay. If he's made arrangements to sell it to another—"

"*No.*" The word is fast and firm and entirely unexpected. "It's not like that. My dad doesn't play games with clients."

"That's true. He doesn't." His brow creases as he looks around the shop, taking in the open boxes, half filled with inventory, the colored sticky notes I've been using to informally assign items to numbered boxes, and the general disarray of the space. "Callie. What's happened to your father?"

It is the way he says my name that loosens my tongue. Had he simply asked the question, I probably would have told him that he could come back in the morning and we'd search the computerized inventory for the piece he's looking for. But there is something so intimate about my name on his lips that I can't help but answer honestly.

"My dad had a stroke last week." My voice hitches as I speak, and I look off toward the side of the store, too wrecked to meet his eyes directly.

"Oh, Callie." He steps closer and takes my hand, and I'm surprised to find that I not only don't pull away, but that I actually have to fight the urge to pull our joint hands close to my heart.

"I didn't know," he says. "I'm so sorry. How is he doing?"

"N-not very well." I suck in a breath and try to gather myself, but it's just so damn hard. My mom walked out when I was four, saying that being a mother was too much responsibility, and ever since I've been my dad's entire world. It's always amazed me that he didn't despise me. But he really doesn't. He says that I was a gift, and I know it's true because I have seen and felt it every day of my life.

Whatever the cause of my disconnect with men, it doesn't harken back to my dad, a little fact that I know fascinates my shrink, though she's too much the professional to flat out tell me as much.

"Does he have decent care? Do you need any referrals? Any help financially?" Raine is crouching in front of me, and I realize that I have sunk down, so that my butt is on the cold tile floor and I am hugging my knees.

I shake my head, a bit dazed to realize this stranger is apparently offering to help pay my dad's medical bills. "We're fine. He's got great care and great insurance. He's just—" I break off as my voice cracks. "*Shit.*"

"Hey, it's okay. Breathe now. That's it, just breathe." He presses his hands to my shoulders, and his face is just inches away. His eyes are wide and safe and warm, and I want to slide into them. To just disappear into a place where there are neither worries nor responsibilities. Where someone strong will hold me and take care of me and make everything bad disappear.

But that's impossible, and so I draw another breath in time with his words and try once again to formulate a coherent thought. "He's—he's got good doctors, really. But he's not lucid. And this is my dad. I mean, Oliver Sinclair hasn't gone a day in his life without an opinion or a witticism."

I feel the tears well in my eyes and I swipe them away with a brusque brush of my thumb. "And it kills me because I can look at him and it breaks my heart to know that he must have all this stuff going on inside his head that he just can't say, and—and—"

But I can't get the words out, and I feel the tears snaking down my cheeks, and dammit, dammit, *dammit*, I do not want to lose it in front of this man—this stranger who doesn't feel like a stranger.

His grip on my shoulders tightens and he leans toward me.

And then—oh, dear god—his lips are on mine and they are as warm and soft as I'd imagined and he's kissing me so gently and so sweetly that all my worries are just melting away and I'm limp in his arms.

"Shhh. It's okay." His voice washes over me, as gentle and calming as a summer rain. "Everything's going to be okay."

I breathe deep, soothed by the warm sensuality of this stranger's golden voice. Except he isn't a stranger. I may not have met him before today, but somehow, here in his arms, I *know* him.

And that, more than anything, comforts me.

Calmer, I tilt my head back and meet his eyes. It is a soft moment and a little sweet—but it doesn't stay that way. It changes in the space of a glance. In the instant of a heartbeat. And what started out as gentle comfort transforms into fiery heat.

I don't know which of us moves first. All I know is that I have to claim him and be claimed by him. That I have to taste him—consume him. Because in some essential way that I don't fully understand, I know that only this man can quell the need burning inside me, and I lose myself in the hot intensity of his mouth upon mine. Of his tongue demanding entrance, and his lips, hard and demanding, forcing me to give everything he wants to take.

I am limp against him, felled by the onslaught of erotic sparks that his kisses have scattered through me. I am lost in the sensation of his hands stroking my back. Of his chest pressed against my breasts.

But it isn't until I realize that he has pulled me into his lap and that I can feel the hard demand of his erection against my rear that I force myself to escape this sensual reality and scramble backward out of his embrace.

"I'm sorry," I say, my breath coming too hard.

"Callie—" The need I hear in his voice reflects my own, and I clench my hands into fists as I fight against the instinct to move back into his arms.

"No." I don't understand what's happening—this instant heat, like a match striking gasoline. I've never reacted to a man this way before. My skin feels prickly, as if I've been caught in a lightning storm. His scent is all over me. And the taste of him lingers on my mouth.

And oh, dear god, I'm wet, my body literally aching with need, with a primal desire for him to just rip my clothes off and take me right there on the hard, dusty floor.

He's triggered a wildness in me that I don't

understand—and my reaction scares the hell out of me.

"You need to go," I say, and I am astonished that my words are both measured and articulate, as if I'm simply announcing that it is closing time to a customer.

He stays silent, but I shake my head anyway, and hold up a finger as if in emphasis.

"No," I say, in response to nothing. "I don't know anything about this amulet. And now you really need to leave. Please," I add. "Please, Raine. I need you to go."

For a moment he only looks at me. Then he nods, a single tilt of his head in acknowledgment. "All right," he says very softly. "I'll go. But I'm not ever leaving you again."

I stand frozen, as if his inexplicable words have locked me in place. He turns slowly and strides out of the shop without looking back. And when the door clicks into place behind him and I am once again alone, I gulp in air as tears well in my eyes again.

I rub my hands over my face, forgiving myself for this emotional miasma because of all the shit that's happened with my dad. Of course I'm a wreck; what daughter wouldn't be?

Determined to get a grip, I follow his path to the door, then hold onto the knob. I'd come over intending to lock it. But now I have to fight the urge to yank it open and beg him to return.

It's an urge I fight. It's just my grief talking. My fear that I'm about to lose my father, the one person in all the world who is close to me, and so I have clung to a stranger in a desperate effort to hold fast to something.

That, at least, is what my shrink would say. *You're fabricating a connection in order to fill a void. It's what you do, Callie. It's what you've always done when lonely and afraid.*

I nod, telling myself I agree with Kelly's voice in my head.

And I do.

Because I am lonely.

And I am afraid of losing my dad.

But that's not the whole of it. Because there's something else that I'm afraid of, too, though I cannot put my finger on it. A strange sense of something coming. Something dark. Something bad.

And what scares me most is the ridiculous, unreasonable fear that I have just pushed away the one person I need to survive whatever is waiting for me out there in the dark.

Want to read more? Visit the Dark Pleasures page on Julie's website.

TAINTED EXCERPT

Please enjoy the first chapter of *Tainted* (Blood Lily Chronicles, Book 1).

PROLOGUE

. . . And by her hand that which would be open may be closed . . .

—The Prophecy of the Orb

CAN I JUST SAY that dying sucks? All that bullshit about seeing the light and having this final moment of inner peace, blah, blah, blah. It's crap.

Dying is messy and terrifying and it hurts like hell.

I ought to know. After all, I was the one on that basement floor in a puddle of my own blood and bile. And there was no peace, no light, no anything. Nothing except the ice-cold knowledge that the sins I'd racked up in the last twelve or so hours were more than sufficient to push me through the gates of hell.

Forget everything else I'd done in my twenty-six years on this earth, good and bad. You go out planning to kill a man—even a man as vile as Lucas Johnson—and your fate is pretty much sealed.

From a practical standpoint, the moment of death is a little bit late to start getting all profound and reflective. As they say, what's done is done. But that doesn't matter, because even if you're the least introspective person on the planet, you still go through the whole Psych 101 rigmarole. You tell yourself that maybe you should have said your bedtime prayers once in a while. You wonder if all those torture-porn horror movies you watched while your boyfriend copped a feel weren't actually a sneak peek into what hell had to offer.

In other words, you get scared.

When you're living, you might tell God to take a flying leap for putting your mother six feet under when you were only fourteen. For leaving you with a stepfather who decided to cuddle up with Jack Daniel's because he no longer had a loving wife in his bed. For leaving you in charge of a pigtailed little half sister who thought you hung the moon.

And for making you arrogant enough to swear that you'd protect that precious kid no matter what, even though that wasn't a promise you could keep. Not when there are monsters like Lucas Johnson trolling the earth. Monsters who suck the life from little girls.

For all those reasons, you might turn your back on God, and think you're oh-so-righteous for doing it. But you'd be wrong.

Trust me. I know.

I know, because even as my life faded, the fires of hell nipped at my toes.

In the end, I got lucky. But then again, luck is all a matter of perspective, isn't it?

CHAPTER ONE

I WOKE UP in total darkness, so out of sorts that I was convinced I'd pulled on the wrong skin along with my blue jeans. Couple that with the fact that anvils were about to split my head wide open, and I think it's fair to say that I wasn't having a good time. I tried to roll over and get my bearings, but even the tiniest movement kicked the hammers in my head to triple-time, and I abandoned the effort before I even got started.

"Fucking A," I said, and immediately wished I hadn't. I'm no American Idol contestant, but my voice doesn't usually inflict extreme pain. Today, it did.

Today? Like I even knew what day it was. Or where I was. Or, for that matter, why I was.

I'd died, after all.

Hadn't I?

Disoriented, I lurched up, only to be halted before I'd barely moved.

I tried again, and realized my wrists and ankles were firmly tied down. What the——?

My heart pounded against my rib cage, but I told myself I wasn't afraid. A big hairy lie, but it was worth a try. I mean, I lied to myself all the time, right? Sometimes I even believed my own shit.

Not this time. I might have dropped out of high school, but I know when to be scared, and tied up in the dark is definitely one of those times. There was no nice, cozy explanation for my current sitch. Instead, my mind filled with high-def NC-17 images of a long, thin blade and a twisted expression of cruel delight painted on a face I knew only too well. Lucas Johnson.

Because this had to be about revenge. Payback for what I'd tried to do. And now I was going to die at the hand of the man I'd gone out to kill.

No, no, no.

No way was I dying. Not now. Not when I'd

survived this far.

I didn't have a clue why I was still alive—I remembered the knife; I remembered the blood. But here I was, living and breathing and, yeah, I was a little immobile at the moment, but I was alive. And I intended to stay that way.

No way was I leaving my little sister to the mercy of the son of a bitch who'd raped and brutalized her. Who'd sent her black roses and mailed erotic postcards. All anonymous. All scary as hell. She would see him in stores, lurking around corners, and by the time she screamed for help, he was gone.

The cops had nailed his sorry ass, but when the system had tossed him on a technicality, I watched Rose come close to losing it every single day. I couldn't stand the thought that the system had kicked the monster free when he should have been in a cage, locked away so he couldn't hurt any more little girls. So he couldn't hurt Rose.

So I'd stolen the gun. I'd tracked him down. And God help me, I'd fired.

At the time, I thought I'd hit him square in

the chest. But I must have missed, because I could remember Johnson rushing me. After that, things were blurrier. I remembered the terror of knowing that I was dying, and I recalled a warm flood of hope. But I had no clue what had happened between warm, fuzzy hope and the cold, hard slab that made up my current reality.

I peered into the darkness again, and this time the velvet curtain seemed to be lifting. The room, I realized, wasn't completely black. Instead, there was a single candle against the far wall, its small flame gathering strength against the blackness.

I stared, puzzled. I was certain there'd been no flame earlier.

Slowly, the area around me shifted into a reddish gray with dark and light spots contrasting to reveal a line of angular symbols painted above the candlestick.

My eyes locked on the symbols, and the trembling started up again. Something was off, and I was overwhelmed by the frantic, urgent fear that the monster I knew was nowhere nearby, and that when I saw what I was *really* up against, I'd desperately wish it were Johnson's sorry ass that was after me.

A cold chill raced up my spine. I wanted the hell out of there.

I was about to start thrashing again—in the desperate hope that the ties would miraculously loosen—when I heard the metallic screech of a creaking hinge. I froze, my breathing shallow, my muscles tense.

The creak intensified and a shaft of anorexic light swept wide across the room as the door arced open. A huge shadow filled the gap. A dark, monstrous form was silhouetted in the doorway, emitting a scent that made me almost vomit.

A monster. And not of the Lucas Johnson variety.

No, Lucas Johnson was a Boy Scout compared to the putrid creature that lumbered forward, bending so that it could fit through the door frame. It lurched toward me, muscles rolling under an elephant-like hide. The creature wore no clothing, and even in the dark, I could see the parasites living in slime inside the folds of skin. Could hear them scurry for safety when the beast moved toward me.

The fetid smell that preceded it made me gag, and I struggled to sink into the stone slab as the beast peered down at me, a string of snot hanging precariously from the orifice that served as a nose.

The creature's mouth twisted, dry skin cracking as the muscles underneath moved, thin lines of blood and pus oozing out from the newly formed fissures. It swaggered to the candle, then leaned over and breathed on the flame. As if its breath were gas, fire leaped into the air, painting the wall with flame and making the symbols glow.

I cried out in alarm and pain, my body suddenly burning from within—the sensation passing as quickly as it had come.

The beast turned to sneer at me. "You," it croaked. Black piggy eyes lit with fury as it brandished a short, bloodied dagger. "Now we finish this business."

A piercing shriek split the dark, and I realized the sound was coming from me. Fire shot through my limbs, and I jerked upright with a fresh burst of determination. To my surprise and relief, I managed to rip my arms free, the ties flapping from my wrists like useless wings.

The creature paused, drawing itself up to its full height. It took a step backward, then dropped to its knees and held its clawed hands high. With the dagger, it sliced its palm, then let the thick, black liquid that flowed from the wound drip into its open mouth. "I serve the Dark Lord, my Master," it said, the words as rough as tires on gravel. "For my sacrifice, I will be rewarded."

The "sacrifice" thing totally freaked me out, but I took advantage of this quaint little monster ritual to reach down and tear at the ties that still bound my ankles. As I did, I noticed that I was wearing a silky white gown, most definitely not the jeans and T-shirt I'd left the house in.

Not that I had time to mull over such fascinating fashion tidbits. Instead, I focused on the business at hand: getting the hell out of there.

About the time I finished ripping, the creature finished praying. It barreled toward me, dagger outstretched. I rolled over, hiking up the skirt as I kicked up and off the slab to land upright beside it. There's probably a name for a move like that, but I didn't know it. Hell, I didn't even know that my body would move like that.

I didn't waste time savoring my new acrobatic persona; instead, I raced for the door. Or, at least, I started to. The sight of the Hell Beast looming there sort of turned me off that plan. Which left me with no choice but to whip around and try to find another exit.

Naturally, there wasn't one.

No, no, no. So far, I had survived the most screwed-up, freaky day of my life, and I wasn't giving up now. And if that meant I fought the disgusting Hell Beast, then dammit, that was just what I was going to do.

The beast must have had the same idea, because as soon as I turned back toward the door, it lashed out, catching me across the face with the back of its massive, clawed hand. The blow sent me hurtling, and I crashed against the huge brass candlestick, causing it to tumble down hard on my rib cage.

Hot wax burned into my chest, but I had no time to reflect on the pain. The beast was on top of me. I did the only thing I could. I grabbed the stick and thrust it upward. The beast weighed a ton, but I must have had decent leverage, because I managed to catch him under the chin with the stick, knocking his head back and eliciting a howl that almost burst my eardrums.

Not being an idiot, I didn't wait around for him to recover. The candlestick was too heavy to carry as a weapon, so I dropped it and ran like hell toward the door, hoping the beast was alone.

I stumbled over the threshold, never so happy to be in a dark, dank hallway. The only light came from medieval-looking candleholders lining the walls every eight or so feet, but as I wasn't sightseeing, the lack of light didn't bother me much. All I wanted was out of there. So I raced on, down musty corridors and around tight corners until finally—*finally*—I slammed into the push bar of a fire door. An alarm screamed into the night as the thick metal door burst open, and I slid out, my nose crinkling as I caught the nasty smell of rotting food, carried on the cool autumn air. I was in an alley, and as my eyes adjusted, I turned to the right and raced toward the street and the safety of the world.

It wasn't until I reached the intersection of the alley and an unfamiliar street that I paused to turn back. The alley was silent. No monsters. No creatures. No boogeymen out to get me.

The street was silent as well. No people or traffic. The streetlights blinking. Late, I thought. And my next thought was to run some more. I would have, too, if I hadn't looked down and noticed my feet in the yellow glow of the street-lamps.

I blinked, confused. Because those didn't look like my feet. And now that I thought about it, my hands and legs seemed all wrong, too. And the bloom of red I now saw on the breast of the white gown completely freaked me out. Which, when you considered the overall circumstances, was saying a lot. Because on the whole, this experience was way, way, way trippy, and the only thing I could figure was that someone had drugged me and I was in the middle of one monster of a hallucination.

Then again, maybe the simplest explanation was the right one: I was losing my mind.

"You're not."

I spun around and found myself looking down on a squat little man in a green overcoat and a battered brown fedora. At least a head shorter than me, he was looking up at me with eyes that would have been serious were they not so amphibian.

"You're not losing it," the frog-man clarified, which suggested to me that I was. Losing it, I mean. After all, the strange little man had just read my mind.

He snorted. "That doesn't make you crazy. Just human."

"Who the devil are you?" I asked, surprised to find that my voice worked, though it sounded somewhat off. I glanced up and down the street, calculating my odds of getting away. Surely I could run faster than this—

"No need to run," he said. Then he stepped off the sidewalk and into the street. As if it had been waiting for his cue, a sleek black limousine pulled to the curb. Frog-man opened the rear door and nodded. "Hop in."

I took a step backward. "Get lost, dickwad."

"Come on, kid. We need to talk. And I know you must be tired. You've had a hell of a day." He nodded down the alley. "You did good in there. But next time remember that you're supposed to kill them. Not give 'em a headache. *Capisce?*"

I most definitely did *not capisce*. "Next time?" I pointed back down the alley. "You had something to do with that? No way," I said, taking another step backward. "No freaking way."

"It's a lot to take in, I know." He opened the door wider. "Why don't you get in, Lily? We really should talk."

My name echoed through the night I looked around, wary, but there was no one else around. "I want answers, you son of a bitch."

He shook his head, and I could imagine him muttering, *tsk*, *tsk*. "Hard to believe you're the one all the fuss is about, but the big guy must know what he's doing, right?"

I blinked.

"But look at you, staring at me like I'm talking in Akkadian. To you I probably am. You're exhausted, right? I tell you, jumping right into the testing . . . it's just not the best method." He shook his head, and this time the *tsk, tsk* actually emerged. "But do they ask me? No. I mean, who am I? Just old Clarence, always around to help. It's enough to give a guy an inferiority complex." He patted my shoulder, making contact before I could pull away. "Don't you worry. This can all wait until tomorrow."

"What testing? What's tomorrow? And who are you?"

"All in good time. Right now," he said, "I'm taking you home."

And before I could ask how he planned to manage that, because I had no intention of getting into the limo with him, he reached over and tapped me on the forehead. "Go to sleep, pet. You need the rest."

I wanted to protest, but couldn't. My eyes closed, and the last thing I remember was his amphibian grin as my knees gave out and I fell to the sidewalk at the frog-man's feet.

Want to read more? Visit the Blood Lily Chronicles page on my website!

CARPE DEMON EXCERPT

Please enjoy this excerpt from Carpe Demon
(you can learn more at my website!)

MY NAME IS KATE CONNOR and I used to be a Demon Hunter.

I've often thought that would be a great pickup line at parties, but with a teenager, a toddler, and a husband, I'm hardly burning up the party circuit. And, of course, the whole demon-hunting thing is one great big gargantuan secret. No one knows. Not my kids, not my husband, and certainly not folks at these imaginary parties where I'm regaling sumptuous hunks with tales from my demon-slaying, vampire-hunting, zombie-killing days.

Back in the day, I was pretty cool. Now I'm a glorified chauffeur for drill-team practice and Gymboree playdates. Less sex appeal, maybe, but I gotta admit I love it. I wouldn't trade my family for anything. And after fourteen years of doing the mommy thing, my demon-hunting skills aren't exactly sharp.

All of which explains why I didn't immediately locate and terminate the demon wandering the pet-food aisle of the San Diablo Wal-Mart. Instead, when I caught a whiff of that telltale stench, I naturally assumed it emanated exclusively from the bottom of a particularly cranky two-year-old. My two-year-old, to be exact.

"Mom! He did it again. What are you feeding him?" That from Alison, my particularly cranky fourteen-year-old. She, at least, didn't stink.

"Entrails and goat turds," I said absently. I sniffed the air again. Surely that was only Timmy I was smelling.

"Mo-*om*." She managed to make the word two syllables. "You don't have to be gross."

"Sorry." I concentrated on my kids, pushing my suspicions firmly out of my mind. I was being silly. San Diablo had been demon-free for years. That's why I lived here, after all.

Besides, the comings and goings of demons weren't my problem anymore. Nowadays my problems leaned more toward the domestic rather than the demonic. Grocery shopping, budgeting, carpooling, mending, cleaning, cooking, parenting, and a thousand other "-ings." All the basic stuff that completely holds a family together and is taken entirely for granted by every person on the planet who doesn't happen to be a wife and stay-at-home mom. (And two points to you if you caught that little bit of vitriol. I'll admit to having a few issues about the whole topic, but, dammit, I work hard. And believe me, I'm no stranger to hard work. It was never easy, say, cleaning out an entire nest of evil, bloodthirsty preternatural creatures with only a few wooden stakes, some holy water, and a can of Diet Coke. But I always managed. And it was a hell of a lot easier than getting a teenager, a husband, and a toddler up and moving in the morning. Now, *that's* a challenge.)

While Timmy fussed and whined, I swung the shopping cart around, aiming for the back of the store and a diaper-changing station. It would have been a refined, fluid motion if Timmy hadn't taken the opportunity to reach out with those chubby little hands. His fingers collided with a stack of Fancy Feast cans and everything started wobbling.

I let out one of those startled little "oh!" sounds, totally pointless and entirely ineffectual. There was a time when my reflexes were so sharp, so perfectly attuned, that I probably could have caught every one of those cans before they hit the ground. But that Kate wasn't with me in Wal-Mart, and I watched, helpless, as the cans clattered to the ground.

Another fine mess ...

Alison had jumped back as the cans fell, and she looked with dismay at the pile. As for the culprit, he was suddenly in a fabulous mood, clapping wildly and screaming "Big noise! Big noise!" while eyeing the remaining stacks greedily. I inched the cart farther away from the shelves.

"Allie, do you mind? I need to go change him."

She gave me one of those put-upon looks that are genetically coded to appear as soon as a girl hits her teens.

"Take your pick," I said, using my most reasonable mother voice. "Clean up the cat food, or clean up your brother."

"I'll pick up the cans," she said, in a tone that perfectly matched her expression.

I took a deep breath and reminded myself that she was fourteen. Raging hormones. Those difficult adolescent years. More difficult, I imagined, for me than for her. "Why don't I meet you in the music aisle. Pick out a new CD and we'll add it to the pile."

Her face lit up. "Really?"

"Sure. Why not?" Yes, yes, don't even say it. I know "why not." Setting a bad precedent, not defining limits, blah, blah, blah. Throw all that psycho mumbo jumbo at me when *you're* wandering Wal-Mart with two kids and a list of errands as long as your arm. If I can buy a day's worth of cooperation for $14.99, then that's a deal I'm jumping all over. I'll worry about the consequences in therapy, thank you very much.

I caught another whiff of nastiness right before we bit the restrooms. Out of habit, I looked around. A feeble old man squinted at me from over the Wal-Mart Sunday insert, but other than him, there was nobody around but me and

Timmy.

"P.U.," Timmy said, then flashed a toothy grin.

I smiled as I parked the shopping cart outside of the ladies' room. "P.U." was his newest favorite word, followed in close second by "Oh, man!" The "Oh, man!" I can blame on Nickelodeon and *Dora the Explorer*. For the other, I lay exclusive blame on my husband, who has never been keen on changing dirty diapers and has managed, I'm convinced, over the short term of Timmy's life, to give the kid a complete and utter complex about bowel movements.

"You're P.U.," I said, hoisting him onto the little dropdown changing table. "But not for long. We'll clean you up, powder that bottom, and slap on a new diaper. You're gonna come out smelling like a rose, kid."

"Like a rose!" he mimicked, reaching for my earrings while I held him down and stripped him.

After a million wipes and one fresh diaper, Timmy was back in the shopping cart. We fetched Allie away from a display of newly released CDs, and she came more or less willingly, a Natalie Imbruglia CD clutched in her hand.

Ten minutes and eighty-seven dollars later I was strapping Timmy into his car seat while Allie loaded our bags into the minivan. As I was maneuvering through the parking lot, I caught one more glimpse of the old man I'd seen earlier. He was standing at the front of the store, between the Coke machines and the plastic kiddie pools, just staring out toward me. I pulled over. My plan was to pop out, say a word or two to him, take a good long whiff of his breath, and then be on my way.

I had my door half open when music started blasting from all six of the Odyssey's speakers at something close to one hundred decibels. I jumped, whipping around to face Allie, who was already fumbling for the volume control and muttering, "Sorry, sorry."

I pushed the power button, which ended the Natalie Imbruglia surround-sound serenade, but did nothing about Timmy, who was now bawling his eyes out, probably from the pain associated with burst eardrums. I shot Allie a stern look, unfastened my seat belt, and climbed into the backseat, all the while trying to make happy sounds that would calm my kid.

"I'm sorry, Mom," Allie said. To her credit she sounded sincere. "I didn't know the volume was up that high." She maneuvered into the backseat on the other side of Timmy and started playing peekaboo with Boo Bear, a bedraggled blue bear that's been Timmy's constant companion since he was five months old. At first Timmy ignored her, but after a while he joined in, and I felt a little surge of pride for my daughter.

"Good for you," I said.

She shrugged and kissed her brother's forehead.

I remembered the old man and reached for the door, but as I looked out at the sidewalk, I saw that he was gone.

"What's wrong?" Allie asked.

I hadn't realized I was frowning, so I forced a smile and concentrated on erasing the worry lines from my forehead. "Nothing," I said. And then, since that was the truth, I repeated myself, "Nothing at all."

FOR THE NEXT THREE HOURS we bounced from store to store as I went down my list for the day: bulk goods at Wal-Mart—*check;* shoes for Timmy at Payless—*check;* Happy Meal for Timmy to ward off crankiness—*check;* new shoes for Allie from DSW—*check;* new ties for Stuart from T.J. Maxx—*check.* By the time we hit the grocery store, the Happy Meal had worn off, both Timmy and Allie were cranky, and I wasn't far behind. Mostly, though, I was distracted.

That old man was still on my mind, and I was irritated with myself for not letting the whole thing drop. But something about him bugged me. As I pushed the shopping cart down the dairy aisle, I told myself I was being paranoid. For one thing, demons tend not to infect the old or feeble. (Makes sense when you think about it; if you're going to suddenly become corporeal, you might as well shoot for young, strong, and virile.) For another, I'm pretty sure there'd been no demon stench, just a particularly pungent toddler diaper. Of course, that didn't necessarily rule out demon proximity. All the demons I'd ever run across tended to pop breath mints like candy, and one even owned the majority share of stock in a mouthwash manufacturer. Even so, common sense told me there was no demon.

Mostly, though, I needed to drop the subject simply because it wasn't my problem anymore. I may have been a Level Four Demon Hunter once upon a time, but that time was fifteen years ago. I was retired now. Out of the loop. Even more, I was out of practice.

I turned down the cookie-and-chips aisle, careful not to let Timmy see as I tossed two boxes of Teddy Grahams into the cart. In the next aisle, Allie lingered in front of the breakfast cereal, and I could practically see her mind debating between the uber-healthy Kashi and her favorite Lucky Charms. I tried to focus on my grocery list (were we really out of All-Bran?), but my brain kept coming back to the old man.

Surely I was just being paranoid. I mean, why would a demon willingly come to San Diablo, anyway? The California coastal town was built on a hillside, its crisscross of streets leading up to St. Mary's, the cathedral that perched at the top of the cliffs, a focal point for the entire town. In addition to being stunningly beautiful, the cathedral was famous for its holy relics, and it drew both tourists and pilgrims. The devout came to San Diablo for the same reason the demons stayed away—the cathedral was holy ground. Evil simply wasn't welcome there.

That was also the primary reason Eric and I had retired in San Diablo. Ocean views, the fabulous California weather, and absolutely no demons or other nasties to ruin our good time. San Diablo was a great place to have kids, friends, and the normal life he and I had both craved. Even now, I thank God that we had ten good years together.

"Mom?" Allie squeezed my free hand, and I realized I'd wandered to the next aisle, and was now holding a freezer door open, staring blankly at a collection of frozen pizzas. "You okay?" From the way her nose crinkled, I knew she suspected I was thinking about her dad.

"Fine," I lied, blinking furiously. "I was trying to decide between pepperoni or sausage for dinner tonight, and then I got sidetracked thinking about making my own pizza dough."

"The last time you tried that, you got dough stuck on the light fixture and Stuart had to climb up and dig it out."

"Thanks for reminding me." But it had worked; we'd both moved past our melancholy. Eric had died just after Allie's ninth birthday, and although she and Stuart got along famously, I knew she missed her dad as much as I did. We talked about it on occasion, sometimes remembering the funny times, and sometimes, like when we visited the cemetery, the memories were filled with tears. But now wasn't the time for either, and we both knew it.

I squeezed her hand back. My girl was growing up. Already she was looking out for me, and it was sweet and heartbreaking all at the same time. "What do you think?" I asked. "Pepperoni?"

"Stuart likes sausage better," she said.

"We'll get both," I said, knowing Allie's distaste for sausage pizza. "Want to rent a movie on the way home? We'll have to look fast so the food doesn't spoil, but surely there's something we've been wanting to see."

Her eyes lit up. "We could do a Harry Potter marathon."

I stifled a grimace. "Why not? It's been at least a month since our last HP marathon."

She rolled her eyes, then retrieved Timmy's sippy cup and adjusted Boo Bear. I knew I was stuck.

My cell phone rang. I checked the caller ID, then leaned against the grocery cart as I answered. "Hey, hon."

"I'm having the day from hell," Stuart said, which was a poor choice of words considering that got me thinking about demons all over again. "And I'm afraid I'm going to ruin your day, too."

"I can hardly wait."

"Any chance you were planning something fabulous for dinner? Enough to serve eight, with cocktails before and some fancy dessert after?"

"Frozen pizza and Harry Potter," I said, certain I knew where this was going to end up.

"Ah," Stuart said. In the background I could hear the eraser end of his pencil tapping against his desktop. Beside me, Allie pretended to bang her head against the glass freezer door. "Well, that would serve eight," he said. "But it may not have quite the cachet I was hoping for."

"It's important?"

"Clark thinks it is." Clark Curtis was San Diablo's lame duck county attorney, and he favored my husband to step into his shoes. Right now, Stuart had a low political profile, working for peanuts as an assistant county attorney in the real estate division. Stuart was months away from formally announcing, but if he wanted to have any hope of winning the election, he needed to start playing the political game, shaking hands, currying favors, and begging campaign contributions. Although a little nervous, he was excited about the campaign, and flattered by Clark's support. As for me, the thought of being a politician's wife was more than a little unnerving.

"A house full of attorneys," I said, trying to think what the heck I could feed them. Or, better yet, if there was any way to get out of this.

Allie sank down to the floor, her back against the freezer, her forehead on her knees.

"And judges."

"Oh, great." This was the part about domesticity that I didn't enjoy. Entertaining just isn't my thing. I hated it, actually. Always had, always would. But my husband, the aspiring politician, loved me anyway. Imagine that.

"I tell you what. I'll have Joan call some caterers. You don't have to do anything except be home by six to meet them. Folks are coming at seven, and I'll be sure to be there by six-thirty to give you a hand."

Now, see? That's why I love him. But I couldn't accept. Guilt welled in my stomach just from the mere suggestion. This was the man I loved, after all. And I couldn't be bothered to pull together a small dinner party? What kind of a heartless wench was I?

"How about rigatoni?" I asked, wondering which was worse, heartless wench or guilty sucker. "And a spinach salad? And I can pick up some appetizers and the stuff for my apple tart." That pretty much exhausted my guest-worthy repertoire, and Stuart knew it.

"Sounds perfect," he said. "But are you sure? It's already four."

"I'm sure," I said, not sure at all, but it was his career, not mine, that was riding on my culinary talents.

"You're the best," he said. "Let me talk to Allie."

I passed the phone to my daughter, who was doing a good impression of someone so chronically depressed she was in need of hospitalization. She lifted a weary hand, took the phone, and pressed it to her ear. "Yeah?"

While they talked, I focused my attention on Timmy, who was being remarkably good. "Nose!" he said when I pointed to my nose. "Ear!" I pointed to my other ear.

"More ear!" The kid was literal, that was for sure. I leaned in close and gave him big wet sloppy kisses on his neck while he giggled and kicked.

With my head cocked to the side like that, I caught a glimpse of Allie, who no longer looked morose. If anything, she looked supremely pleased with herself. I wondered what she and Stuart were scheming, and suspected it was going to involve me carpooling a load of teenage girls to the mall.

"What?" I asked as Allie hung up.

"Stuart said it was okay with him if I spent the night at Mindy's. Can I? Please?"

I ran my fingers through my hair and tried not to fantasize about killing my husband. The reasonable side of me screamed that he was only trying to help. The annoyed side of me retorted that he'd just sent my help packing, and I now had to clean the house, cook dinner, and keep Timmy entertained all on my own.

"Pleeeeeeze?"

"Fine. Sure. Great idea." I started pushing the cart toward the dairy aisle while Timmy babbled something entirely unintelligible. "You can get your stuff and head to Mindy's as soon as we get home."

She did a little hop-skip number, then threw her arms around my neck. "Thanks, Mom! You're the best"

"Mmmm. Remember this the next time you're grounded."

She pointed at her chest, her face ultra-innocent "Me? In trouble? I think you have me confused with some other daughter."

I tried to scowl, but didn't quite manage it, and she knew she'd won me over. Well, what the heck? I was a woman of the new millennium. I'd staked vampires, defeated demons, and incapacitated incubi. How hard could a last-minute dinner party be?

MINDY DUPONT LIVES at our exact address, only one street over. Once the girls became inseparable, Laura Dupont and I followed suit, and now she's more like a sister than a neighbor. I knew she wouldn't care if Allie stayed over, so I didn't bother calling ahead. I just bought a chocolate cake for bribery/thank-you purposes, then added it to Allie's pile as she set off across our connecting backyards to Laura's patio. (They're not technically connected. A paved city easement runs between us, and it's fenced off on both sides. Last year Stuart convinced the city that they should install gates on either side, so as to facilitate any city workers who might need to get back there. I've never once seen a utility man wandering behind my house, but those gates have sure made life easier for me, Laura, and the girls. Have I mentioned I adore my husband?)

A little less than ten minutes later I had Timmy settled in front of a *Wiggles* video, and I was pushing a dust mop over our hardwood floors, trying to get all the nooks and crannies a judge might notice, and ignoring all the other spots. I was pretty certain there was a dust bunny convention under the sofa, but until the conventioneers started wandering out into the rest of the house, I wasn't going to worry about it.

The phone rang, and I lunged for it.

"Allie says you're doing the dinner party thing. Need help?"

"Actually, I'm good. My clothes are laid out, the sauce is simmering, the appetizers are on cookie sheets ready to go in the oven, and I even managed to find eight wineglasses." I took a deep breath. "And they match."

"Well, aren't you just a little Martha Stewart? In the pre-scandal, domestic-goddess days, of course. And the munchkin?"

"In his jammies in front of the television."

"All finished with bathtime?"

"No bath. Extra videos."

She released a long-suffering sigh. "Finally, a flaw. Now I don't have to hate you after all."

I laughed. "Hate me all you want for managing to pull this together. It's a feat worthy of your hatred." I didn't point out that I hadn't actually pulled it off yet. I wasn't counting this evening as a success until the guests went home happy, patting their tummies and promising Stuart all sorts of political favors. "Just don't hate me for dumping Allie on you. You sure it's okay?"

"Oh, yeah. They're locked in Mindy's room trying out all my Clinique samples. If they get bored, we'll go get ice cream. But I don't see boredom in their future. I've got two years' worth of samples in that box. I figure that works out to at least four hours of free time. I'm going to make some popcorn, stick in one of my old Cary Grant videos, and wait up for Paul."

"Oh, sure, rub it in," I said.

She laughed. "You've got your own Cary Grant"

"And he'll be home soon. I'd better run."

She clicked off after making me promise to call if I needed anything. But for once, I actually had it under control. Amazing. I tucked the dust mop in the utility closet, then headed back to take a final look at the living room. Comfortable and presentable. Some might even say it had a casual elegance. The dancing dinosaur on the television screen really didn't add to the ambience, but I'd close up the entertainment center as soon as Timmy went to bed.

I was running through my mental checklist as I headed back into the kitchen. A flash of movement outside the kitchen window caught my attention, and I realized I'd forgotten to feed Kabit, our cat.

I considered waiting until after the party, decided that wasn't fair, then crossed to the breakfast area where we keep the cat food bowl on a little mat next to the table. I'd just bent to pick up the water dish when the sound of shattering glass filled the room.

I was upright almost instantly, but that wasn't good enough. The old man from Wal-Mart bounded through the wrecked window, surprisingly agile for an octogenarian, and launched himself at me. We tumbled to the ground, rolling across the floor and into the actual kitchen, until we finally came to a stop by the stove. He was on top of me, his bony hands pinning down my wrists, and his face over mine. His breath reeked of rancid meat and cooked cauliflower, and I made a vow to never, *ever* ignore my instincts again.

"Time to die, Hunter," he said, his voice low and breathy and not the least bit old-sounding.

A little riffle of panic shot through my chest. He shouldn't know I used to be a Hunter. I was retired. New last name. New hometown. This was bad. And his words concerned me a heck of a lot more than the kill-fever I saw in his eyes.

I didn't have time to worry about it, though, because the guy was shifting his hands from my wrists to my neck, and I had absolutely no intention of getting caught in a death grip.

As he shifted his weight, I pulled to the side, managing to free up my leg. I brought it up, catching his groin with my knee. He howled, but didn't let go. That's the trouble with demons;

kneeing them in the balls just doesn't have the effect it should. Which meant I was still under him, smelling his foul breath, and frustrated as hell because I didn't need this shit. I had a dinner to fix.

From the living room, I heard Timmy yelling, "Momma! Momma! Big noise! Big noise!" and I knew he was abandoning the video to come find out where the big noise came from.

I couldn't remember if I'd closed the baby gate, and there was no way my two-year-old was going to see his mom fighting a demon. I might be out of practice, but right then, I was motivated. "I'll be right there!" I yelled, then pulled on every resource in my body and flipped over, managing to hop on Pops. I scraped at his face, aiming for his eyes, but only scratched his skin.

He let out a wail that sounded as if it came straight from the depths of hell, and lurched toward me. I sprang back and up, surprised and at the same time thrilled that I was in better shape than I realized. I made a mental note to go to the gym more often even as I kicked out and caught him in the chin. My thigh screamed in pain, and I knew I'd pay for this in the morning.

Another screech from the demon, this time harmonized by Timmy's cries and the rattle of the baby gate that was, thank God, locked. Pops rushed me, and I howled as he slammed me back against the granite countertops. One hand was tight around my throat, and I struggled to breathe, lashing out to absolutely no effect.

The demon laughed, his eyes filled with so much pleasure that it pissed me off even more. "Useless bitch," he said, his foul breath on my face. "You may as well die, Hunter. You surely will when my master's army rises to claim victory in his name."

That didn't sound good, but I couldn't think about it right then. The lack of oxygen was getting to me. I was confused, my head swimming, everything starting to fade to a blackish purple. But then Timmy's howls dissolved into whimpers. A renewed burst of anger and fear gave me strength. My hand groped along the counter until I found a wineglass. My fingers closed around it, and I slammed it down, managing to break off the base.

The room was starting to swim, and I needed to breathe desperately. I had one chance, and one chance only. With all the strength I could muster I slammed the stem of the wineglass toward his face, then sagged in relief when I felt it hit home, slipping through the soft tissue of his eyeball with very little resistance.

I heard a *whoosh* and saw the familiar shimmer as the demon was sucked out of the old man, and then the body collapsed to my floor. I sagged against my counter, drawing gallons of air into my lungs. As soon as I felt steady again, I focused on the corpse on my newly cleaned floor and sighed. Unlike in the movies, demons don't dissolve in a puff of smoke or ash, and right as I was staring down at the body, wondering how the heck I was going to get rid of it before the party, I heard the familiar squeak of the patio door, and then Allie's frantic voice in the living room. "Mom! Mom!"

Timmy's yelps joined my daughter's, and I closed my eyes and prayed for strength.

"Don't come in here, sweetie. I broke some glass and it's all over the floor." As I talked, I hoisted my dead foe by the underarms and dragged him to the pantry. I slid him inside and slammed the door.

"What?" Allie said, appearing around the corner with Timmy in her arms.

I counted to five and decided this wasn't the time to lecture my daughter about listening or following directions. "I said don't come in here." I moved quickly toward her, blocking her path. "There's glass all over the place."

"Jeez, Mom." Her eyes were wide as she took in the mess that was now my kitchen. "Guess you can't give me any more grief about my room, huh?"

I rolled my eyes.

She glanced at the big picture window behind our breakfast table. The one that no longer had glass. "What happened?"

"Softball," I said. "Just crashed right through."

"Wow. I guess Brian finally hit a homer, huh?"

"Looks that way." Nine-year-old Brian lived next door and played softball in his backyard constantly. I felt a little guilty blaming the mess on him, but I'd deal with that later.

"I'll get the broom."

She plunked Timmy onto his booster seat, then headed for the pantry. I caught her arm. "I'll take care of it, sweetie."

"But you've got the party!"

"Exactly. And that's why I need to be able to focus." That really made no sense, but she didn't seem to notice. "Listen, just put Timmy to bed for me, then head on back to Mindy's. Really. I'll be fine."

She looked unsure. "You're sure?"

"Absolutely. It's all under control. Why'd you come back, anyway?"

"I forgot my new CD."

I should have guessed. I picked Timmy back up (who, thankfully, was quiet now and watching the whole scene with interest). "Put the munchkin down and you'll be doing me a huge favor."

She frowned, but didn't argue as she took Timmy from me.

"Night, sweetie," I said, then gave both her and Timmy a kiss.

She still looked dubious, but she readjusted her grip on Timmy and headed toward the stairs. I let out a little sigh of relief and glanced at the clock. I had exactly forty-three minutes to clean up the mess in my kitchen, dispose of a dead demon, and pull together a dinner party. After that, I could turn my attention to figuring out what a demon was doing in San Diablo. And, more important, why he had attacked *me*.

But first, the rigatoni.

Did I have my priorities straight, or what?

JK'S BOOKLIST

I hope you enjoyed *Find Me in Pleasure*! If you think your friends or other readers would enjoy the book, I'd be honored if you'd rate or "like" the book or leave a review at your favorite retailers. And, of course, I'm always thrilled if you want to spread the word through Twitter, Facebook or other social media outlets.

Questions about the book, or me, or the meaning of the universe? I'd love to hear from you. You can reach me via email at juliekenner@gmail.com or on Twitter (I'm @juliekenner) or through Facebook at www.facebook.com/JulieKennerBooks or www.facebook.com/JKennerBooks

Don't want to miss any of my books or news? Be sure to sign up for my newsletter. You can use this link to the newsletter (http://eepurl.com/-tfoP) or go to my website, www.juliekenner.com

I've written a lot of books, and most of them

are available in digital format. Here's a list of just a few (you can find more at my website!); I hope you check them out!

Kate Connor Demon-Hunting Soccer Mom Series that Charlaine Harris, *New York Times* bestselling author of the Sookie Stackhouse / True Blood series, raved "shows you what would happen if Buffy got married and kept her past a secret. It's a hoot."

Carpe Demon

California Demon

Demons Are Forever

The Demon You Know

Deja Demon

Demon Ex Machina

Pax Demonica

The Trouble with Demons

Learn more at
DemonHuntingSoccerMom.com

The Protector (Superhero) Series that *RT Book Review* magazine raves are true originals, "filled with humor, adventure and fun!"

The Cat's Fancy (prequel)

Aphrodite's Kiss

Aphrodite's Passion

Aphrodite's Secret

Aphrodite's Flame

Aphrodite's Embrace

Aphrodite's Delight

Aphrodite's Charms (boxed set)

Dead Friends and Other Dating Dilemmas

Learn more at WeProtectMortals.com

Blood Lily Chronicles

Tainted

Torn

Turned

The Blood Lily Chronicles (boxed set)

Devil May Care Series

Raising Hell

Sure As Hell

Dark Pleasures

Caress of Darkness

Find Me in Darkness

Find Me in Pleasure

Find Me in Passion

Caress of Pleasure

By J. Kenner as J.K. Beck:

Shadow Keepers Series (dark paranormal romance)

When Blood Calls

When Pleasure Rules

When Wicked Craves

When Passion Lies

When Darkness Hungers

When Temptation Burns

Shadow Keepers: Midnight

As J. Kenner:

New York Times & *USA Today* **bestselling Stark Trilogy (erotic romance)**

Release Me (a *New York Times* and *USA Today* bestseller)

Claim Me (a #2 *New York Times* bestseller!)

Complete Me (a #2 *New York Times* bestseller!)

Take Me (epilogue novella)

Tame Me (A Stark International novella)

Have Me

Say My Name

On My Knees

New York Times & *USA Today* **bestselling** *The Most Wanted* **series (erotic romance)**

Wanted

Heated

Ignited

Thanks again, and happy reading!

ABOUT JULIE

Author Photo by Kathy Whittaker

A *New York Times*, *USA Today*, *Publishers Weekly*, and *Wall Street Journal* bestselling author, Julie Kenner (aka J. Kenner) writes a range of stories including romance (erotic, sexy, funny & sweet), young adult novels, chick lit suspense and paranormal mommy lit. Her foray into the latter, *Carpe Demon: Adventures of a Demon-Hunting Soccer Mom*, was selected as a Booksense Summer Paperback Pick for 2005, was a Target Breakout Book, was a Barnes & Noble Number One

SFF/Fantasy bestseller for seven weeks, and is in development as a feature film with 1492 Pictures.

As J. Kenner, she also writes erotic romance (including the bestselling Stark Trilogy) as well as dark and sexy paranormal romances, including the Shadow Keeper series previously published as J.K. Beck.

You can connect with Julie through her website, www.juliekenner.com, Twitter (@juliekenner) and her Facebook pages at www.facebook.com/juliekennerbooks and www.facebook.com/jkennerbooks.

For all the news on upcoming releases, contests, and other fun stuff, be sure to sign up for her newsletter (http://eepurl.com/-tfoP).

CPSIA information can be obtained
at www.ICGtesting.com
Printed in the USA
LVOW13s1756240817
546242LV00014B/237/P